Oliver Optic

Poor and Proud

The Fortunes of Katy Redburn

Oliver Optic

Poor and Proud
The Fortunes of Katy Redburn
ISBN/EAN: 9783337341305

Printed in Europe, USA, Canada, Australia, Japan

Cover: Foto ©Andreas Hilbeck / pixelio.de

More available books at **www.hansebooks.com**

POOR AND PROUD

OR

THE FORTUNES OF KATY REDBURN

A Story for Young Folks

BY

OLIVER OPTIC

———

THE MERSHON COMPANY

RAHWAY, N. J.   NEW YORK

BY THE SAME AUTHOR

THE BOAT CLUB

NOW OR NEVER

POOR AND PROUD

ALL ABOARD

TRY AGAIN

LITTLE BY LITTLE

———

12mo. Price, 60 cents.

———

THE MERSHON COMPANY

RAHWAY, N. J.   NEW YORK

TO

ALICE MARIE ADAMS

This Book

IS AFFECTIONATELY DEDICATED

BY HER FATHER.

PREFACE.

Bobby Bright and Harry West, whose histories
were contained in the last two volumes of the
" Library for Young Folks," were both smart boys.
The author, very grateful for the genial welcome
extended to these young gentlemen, begs leave to
introduce to his juvenile friends a smart girl,—
Miss Katy Redburn,—whose fortunes, he hopes,
will prove sufficiently interesting to secure their
attention.

If any of my adult readers are disposed to accuse
me of being a little extravagant, I fear I shall have
to let the case go by default; but I shall plead, in
extenuation, that I have tried to be reasonable, even
where a few grains of the romantic element were
introduced; for Baron Munchausen and Sinbad
the Sailor were standard works on my shelf in boy-

hood, and I may possibly have imbibed some of their peculiar spirit. But I feel a lively satisfaction in the reflection that, whatever exaggerations the critic may decide I have perpetrated in this volume, I have made the success of Katy Redburn depend upon her good principles, her politeness, her determined perseverance, and her overcoming that foolish pride which is a snare to the feet. In these respects she is a worthy exemplar for the young.

Pride and poverty do not seem to agree with each other; but there is a pride which is not irreconcilable with the humblest station. This pride of character finds an illustration in the life of my heroine.

· Thanking my young friends again for the pleasant reception given to my former books, I submit this volume in the hope that Katy Redburn will prove to be a worthy and agreeable companion for their leisure hours.

Wᴉʟʟɪᴀᴍ T. Aᴅᴀᴍs.

Dorchester, September 29, 1858.

CONTENTS.

POOR AND PROUD

OR

THE FORTUNES OF KATY REDBURN

CHAPTER I.

KATY REDBURN AND OTHERS ARE INTRODUCED.

"Give me a flounder, Johnny?" said a little girl of eleven, dressed in coarse and ragged garments, as she stooped down and looked into the basket of the dirty young fisherman, who sat with his legs hanging over the edge of the pier.

"I'll bet I won't," replied Johnny gruffly, as he drew the basket out of the reach of the supplicant. "You needn't come round here tryin' to hook my fish."

"You hooked 'em," said another juvenile angler who sat on the capsill of the pier by Johnny's side.

"Who says I hooked 'em?" blustered Johnny, whose little dirty paws involuntarily assumed the form of a pair of fists, scientifically disposed and ready to be the instruments of the owner's vengeance upon the traducer of his character.

"I say so," added Tommy Howard, who did not seem to be at all alarmed at the warlike attitude of his fellow-angler.

"Say it again, and I'll smash your head," continued Johnny, jumping up from his seat.

"Didn't you hear me? Once is enough."

Tommy coolly hauled up a large flounder at that moment, and threw the fish into his basket. It was rather refreshing to see how regardless he was of that pair of menacing fists.

"Jest you say that once more, and see what I'll do," persisted Johnny.

"I won't do it."

"You dasen't say it again."

"Perhaps I dasen't; at any rate, I shan't."

"Do you mean to say I hooked them fish?" exclaimed Johnny, desperately, for it seemed as though he must do something to vindicate his injured honor.

" That's just what I did say."

But Tommy was so confoundedly cool that his fellow-angler had some doubts about the expediency of " pitching into him." Probably a vision of defeat flashed through his excited brain, and discretion seemed the better part of valor. Yet he was not disposed to abandon his position, and advanced a pace or two towards his provoking companion; a movement which, to an unpracticed eye, would indicate a purpose to do something.

" Don't fight, Tommy," said the little ragged girl.

" I don't mean to fight, Katy,"—Johnny, at these words, assumed an artistic attitude, ready to strike the first blow,—" only if Johnny hits me, I shall knock him into the middle of next week."

Johnny did not strike. He was a prudent young man.

"Don't fight, Johnny," repeated the girl, turning to the excited aspirant for the honors of the ring.

"Do you suppose I'll let him tell me I hooked them fish?" blustered Johnny.

"He didn't mean anything."

"Yes I did," interposed Tommy. "He caught 'em on a hook; so of course he hooked 'em. I hooked mine too."

"Is that what you meant?" asked Johnny, a broad grin overspreading his dirty face, and his fist suddenly expanding into dirty paws again.

"That's just what I meant; and your skull is as thick as a two-inch plank, or you would have seen what I meant."

"I see now."

Johnny was not disposed to resent this last insinuation about the solidity of his cranium. He was evidently too glad to get out of the scrape without a broken head or a bloody nose. Johnny was a bully, and he had a bully's reputation to maintain;

but he never fought when the odds were against him; and he had a congressman's skill in backing out before the water got too hot. On the whole, he rather enjoyed the pun; and he had the condescension to laugh heartily, though somewhat unnaturally at the jest.

" Will you give me a flounder, Tommy? " said the little ragged girl, as she glanced into his well-filled basket.

" What do you want of him, Katy? " asked Tommy, turning round and gazing up into her sad, pale face.

Katy hesitated; her bosom heaved, and her lips compressed, as though she feared to answer the question.

" To eat," she replied, at last, in a husky tone.

" What's the matter, Katy? "

The face of the child seemed to wear a load of care and anxiety, and as the young fisherman gazed a tear started from her eye, and slid down her cheek. Tommy's heart melted as he saw this exhibition of sorrow.   He wondered what could ail her.

"My mother is sick," replied Katy, dashing away the telltale tear.

"I know that; but what do you want of flounders?"

"We have nothing to eat now," said Katy, bursting into tears. "Mother has not been able to do any work for more than three months; and we haven't got any money now.   It's all gone.   I haven't had any breakfast to-day."

"Take 'em all, Katy!" exclaimed Tommy, jumping up from his seat on the capsill of the pier. "How will you carry them?   Here, I will string 'em for you."

Tommy was all energy now, and thrust his hands down into the depths of his pockets in search of a piece of twine.   Those repositories of small stores did not contain a string, however; but mixed up with a piece of chalk, a slate pencil, an iron hinge, two marbles, a brass ring, and six inches of stovepipe chain, were two cents, which the owner thereof carefully picked out of the heap of miscellaneous articles and thrust them into the hand of Katy.

"Here, take them; and as you go by the grocery at the corner of the court, buy a two-cent roll," whispered he. "Got a bit o' string, Johnny?" he added aloud, as Katy began to protest against taking the money.

"Haint got none; but I'll give you a piece of my fish line, if you want," replied the bully, who was now unusually obliging.

"There's a piece of spunyarn, that's just the thing I want;" and Tommy ran halfway up the pier to the bridge, picked up the line, and commenced stringing the flounders on it.

"I don't want them all, Tommy; only give me two or three. I never shall forget you, Tommy," said Katy, her eyes suffused with tears of gratitude.

"I'm sorry things go so bad with you, Katy, and I wish I could do something more for you."

"I don't want any thing more. Don't put any

more on the string. There's six. We can't eat any more."

" Well, then, I'll bring you some more to-morrow," replied Tommy, as he handed her the string of fish. " Stop a minute; here's a first-rate tom-cod; let me put him on;" and he took the string and added the fish to his gift.

" I never shall forget you, Tommy; I shall only borrow the two cents; I will pay you again some time," said she, in a low tone, so that Johnny could not hear her.

" Never mind 'em, Katy. Don't go hungry again for a minute. Come to me, and I'll help you to something or other."

" Thank you, Tommy;" and with a lighter heart than she had brought with her, she hastened up the pier, no doubt anticipating a rich feast from the string of fish.

The pier of the new South Boston bridge was then, as now, a favorite resort for juvenile fisher-men. Flounders, tom-cod, and eels, to say nothing of an occasional sculpin, which boys still persist in calling " crahpies," or " crahooners," used to furnish abundant sport to a motley group of youngsters, wherein the sons of merchants mingled democratically with the dirty, ragged children of the " tenfooters " in the vicinity. The pier was neutral ground, and Frederic Augustus made a friend of Michael or Dennis, and probably neither was much damaged by this free companionship; for Michael or Dennis often proves to be more of a gentleman in his rags and dirty face than Frederic Augustus in his broadcloth and white linen.

Katy walked as fast as her little feet would carry her, till she came to a court leading out of Essex Street. The bells were ringing for one o'clock as she entered the grocery at the corner and purchased the two-cent roll which Tommy Howard's bounty enabled her to add to her feast. Elated with the success of her mission, she quickened her pace up the court to a run, rushed into the house and upstairs to her mother's room with as much enthusiasm as though she had found a bag of gold, instead of having obtained a very simple dinner.

"Oh, mother, I've got a lot of flounders and some bread for you!" exclaimed she, as she bolted into the room.

"Then you have money," said a cold voice in the chamber; and Katy perceived, standing near the bed on which her mother lay, a man who was no stranger to her.

It was Dr. Flynch; but let not my young reader make a mistake. He was no good Samaritan, who had come to pour oil and wine into the wounds of the poor sick woman; not even a physician, who had come to give medicine for a fee, to restore her to health and strength. It is true he was called a doctor, and he had been a doctor, but he did not practice the healing art now. If he had failed to make a physician, it was not because his heart was so tender that he could not bear to look upon pain and suffering. He was the agent of Mrs. Gordon, a widow lady, who owned the house in which

Katy's mother lived. He collected her rents, and transacted all her business; and as far as dollars and cents were concerned, he had certainly been a faithful servant. But Dr. Flynch was a prudent and discreet man, and did not hurt the feelings of the good lady who employed him by telling her about the difficulties he encountered in the discharge of his duty, or by describing the harsh and even cruel means to which he was sometimes obliged to resort, in order to obtain the rent of poor tenants.

"Mrs. Redburn," said Dr. Flynch, when he had heard the exclamation of Katy, "you have told me a falsehood. You said you had no money, not a cent. Where did you get that roll, child?"

"At the store at the corner of the court," replied Katy, abashed by the cold dignity of the agent.

"Precisely so, Mrs. Redburn; but you do not buy bread without money. You have attempted to deceive me. I have pitied you up to the present time, and indulged you in the non-payment of your rent for over a week.   I can do so no longer, for you have told me a falsehood."

"No, sir, I have not," pleaded the sick woman.

"Your child buys bread."

"I did not give her the money."

"Where did you get the money to buy that roll with?" demanded Dr. Flynch, turning sharply to Katy.

"Tommy Howard gave it to me."

"Who is Tommy Howard?"

"He lives on the other side of the court."

"Very probable that a dirty, ragged boy gave her the money! This is another falsehood, Mrs. Redburn.   I lament that a person in your situation should have no higher views of Christian morality than to lie yourself, and teach your child to lie, which is much worse."

The poor woman burst into tears, and protested that she had told the truth, and nothing but the truth; declaring that Katy was a good girl, that she had eaten nothing that day, and would not tell a lie.   Dr. Flynch was a man of method, and when a tenant did not pay the rent, it was his purpose to get rid of that tenant in the quietest way possible. In the present case there was a difficulty, and public opinion would not justify him in turning a sick woman out of the house; but if she lied, had money concealed and would not pay her rent, it would alter the matter.   As he wished to believe this was the case, he had no difficulty in convincing himself, and thus quieting his poor apology for a conscience.

Besides being a man of method, Dr. Flynch was a man of upright walk and conversation; at least, he passed for such with those who did not know anything about him.   If Mrs. Gordon should happen to hear that he had turned out the sick woman, he could then inform her how feelingly he had pointed out to her the wickedness of her conduct, which he thought would sound exceedingly well.

"Mrs. Redburn," he continued, "I will give you till this time to-morrow to get out of the house;

if you are not gone then, I shall be under the painful necessity of removing your goods into the street. Good-morning!" and Dr. Flynch turned upon his heel, and walked out of the room.

"My poor child! what will become of us?" sobbed the sick woman, as she grasped Katy's hand, and pressed it to her bosom with convulsive energy.

"Don't cry, mother; something can be done. I will go and see Mrs. Gordon, and beg her to let you stay here."

"You must not do that; Dr. Flynch told me if I troubled her about the house, I should not stay in it another minute, even if I paid the rent."

"He is a bad man, mother; and I don't believe Mrs. Gordon knows what he does here."

"There is one thing more we can do, Katy," continued Mrs. Redburn, wiping away her tears, and taking from under her pillow a heavy silver watch. "This was your father's; but we must sell it now. It is all we have left."

"I should hate to have that sold, mother."

"We must sell it, or pawn it."

"We will pawn it then."

"How shall we do it? I have not strength to rise, and they will cheat you if you offer it."

"I will tell you what I can do, mother; I will get Simon Sneed to go with me to the pawnbroker's shop. He is very kind to me, and I know he will. He comes home to dinner at two o'clock."

This plan was agreed to, and Katy then went to work to clean and cook the flounders.

CHAPTER II.

THE HISTORY OF THE SILVER WATCH.

KATY REDBURN was only eleven years old, and not a very accomplished cook; but as the children learn faster in the homes of the poor than in the dwellings of the rich, she had a very tolerable idea of the management of a frying pan. The operation of cleaning the flounders was the greatest trial, for the skin of the fish has to be removed. She cut her fingers with the knife, and scratched and pricked her hands with the sharp bones; but she was resolute, and finally accomplished the task to her entire satisfaction. An occasional direction from her mother enabled her to cook the fish properly, and dinner was ready. There were still a few small stores left in the closet, and Katy made a cup of tea for her mother, and with it placed a delicate little flounder by the side of the bed. The invalid had no appetite; but to please Katy she ate a portion of the fish and bread, though it was very hard work for her to do so. The little girl, gladdened by this unwonted sight, made a hearty meal, without a thought of the trials and sorrows which the future might have in store for them.

When she had put away the dishes, and placed everything in order, she washed herself, combed her hair, sewed up a great rent in her dress, and otherwise attempted to make herself as tidy as possible for the mission she was about to undertake.

"It is not time for you to go yet, Katy; and before the watch is carried off, I want to tell you something about your father, that you may learn to prize it as I do."

Katy seated herself on the side of the bed, for she was very anxious to hear more about her father than she already knew. She had often asked her mother about him, but she had generally evaded her questions, and did not seem willing to tell her all she knew. She thought there was some secret connected with his history, and with a child's curiosity she was eager to have the mystery unfolded. But it was no great secret, after all; only a painful history, which her sensitive mother did not like to rehearse. Mrs. Redburn handed the watch to Katy, and asked her to look upon the back of it.

"Yes, mother, I have often seen those words on there—'ALL FOR THE BEST.' What do they mean?" said Katy.

"This watch was given to your father by my father," replied Mrs. Redburn, with a deep sigh, for the words seemed to recall happy memories of the past.

"Who was your father?" asked the attentive little girl.

"His name was Matthew Guthrie. He was a merchant, in Liverpool, England, where I was born."

"A merchant, mother? Then he was a rich man, and lived in a great house, and had plenty of servants."

" He was rich, and lived in good style. One day there came a young man in great distress to his counting room. He was a clerk, and had been sent by his employer in Manchester to pay a large sum of money to my father. After leaving the train, he had entered an ale house, where he had been robbed of the remittance. He had been imprudent, but instead of running away he went directly to my father, and informed him of his misfortune. The young man felt that he was ruined, but he said he was determined not to leave Liverpool till he had found the money. He was sure he knew the man who had robbed him, and my father procured the services of several policemen to assist him in his search. All that day and all that night, attended by policemen, he visited the resorts of vice and crime, and his perseverance was rewarded with success. He found the man, and the money was recovered. My father was so well pleased with the energy of the young man, that he gave him a situation to his counting room. That young man was John Redburn, your father.   My father gave him a much larger salary than he had been receiving before, so that his misfortune in losing the money proved to be a piece of good fortune to him, for it procured him a much better situation.   The new clerk performed his duties very faithfully, and at the end of a year my father presented him this watch, with the motto ' All for the Best,' in allusion to the manner in which he had obtained his situation."

" But how came you here, mother, if your father was rich, and lived in a fine house?   You are very poor now;" asked Katy, who feared that the mystery was yet to come.

Mrs. Redburn burst into tears, and covered her face with her hands, as the pleasant memories of her former happy home rushed through her mind.

" Don't cry, mother; I won't ask you any more questions," said Katy, grieved to find she had reminded her mother of some unpleasant thing.

" It was all my own fault, Katy.   I am here,

poor and wretched, because I disobeyed my father; because I did what he desired me not to do.   I will tell you all about it, Katy.   I became acquainted with the new clerk, John Redburn, and the result of our acquaintance was, that we were married in about a year.   We ran away from home; for my father, however much he liked John as a clerk, was not willing that he should be my husband.   He forbade John's coming to our house, and forbade my seeing him.   I disobeyed him.   We were married, and John was discharged.   My father refused to see me again."

" That was cruel," interposed Katy.

" My father was right, and I have always regretted that I disobeyed him.   We came to America, and your father procured a situation in New York, where you were born, about a year after we arrived.   For three years we got along very well.   I wish I could stop here, Katy, for the rest of the story is very sad."

" Don't tell me any more, mother; it makes you

feel so bad, I would rather not hear it. I know now why you value the watch so much, and I hope we shall be able to get it back again."

" I fear not. But you must hear the rest of this sad story."

Mrs. Redburn continued the narrative, though tears blinded her eyes, and sobs choked her utterance, as she told of the struggle she had had with poverty and want. Her husband had done very well in New York; and, gay and light-hearted in the midst of his prosperity, his habits had been gradually growing worse and worse, till he lost his situation, and became a common sot. The poor wife had then been compelled to toil for her own support and that of her child; and having been brought up in luxury and ease, it was a dreadful task to her.

John obtained another situation, but soon lost it. He was a good-hearted man when he had not been drinking, and keenly felt the disgrace and misery he was heaping upon himself and his unhappy wife.

Once he had the resolution to abandon the cup, fully determined to redeem his lost character, and make his family happy again. The better to accomplish this, he removed to Boston, where he obtained a good situation, and for more than a year he adhered to his resolution. Mrs. Redburn was happy again, and tremblingly hoped that the clouds of darkness had forever passed away.

The evil time came again, and John Redburn sank down lower than ever before. His wife lost all hope of him, and struggled, with the courage of a hero and the fortitude of a martyr, against the adverse tide that set against her. She was fortunate in obtaining plenty of sewing, and was able to support herself and child very well; but her husband, now lost to all sense of decency, contrived to obtain, from time to time, a portion of her hard earnings. She could never have believed that John Redburn would come to this; for, as a clerk in her father's counting room, he had been all that was good and noble; but there he was, a miserable sot, lost to himself, to his family, and the world.

One morning in winter he was brought home to her dead. He had died in the watch house, of delirium tremens. He was buried, and peace, if not hope, settled on the brow of the broken-hearted wife.

Year after year Mrs. Redburn struggled on, often with feeble hands and fainting heart, to earn a subsistence for herself and Katy. She had been bred in opulence, and her wants were not so few and simple as the wants of those who have never enjoyed the luxury of a soft couch and a well-supplied table. She had never learned that calculating economy which provides a great deal with very small means. Hence it was much harder for her to support herself and child than it would have been for one who had been brought up in a hovel.

She had done very well, however, until, a few months before our story opens, she had been taken sick, and was no longer able to work. Her disease was an affection of the spine, which was at times very painful, and confined her to the bed.

"But where is your father now?" asked Katy, when her mother had finished the narrative.

"I do not know; if he is alive, he probably lives in Liverpool."

"Why don't you write a letter to him?"

"I have done so several times, but have never received any reply. I wrote shortly after your father died, giving an account of my situation. I am sure my father never could have got my letter, or he would have answered me. I know he would not let me suffer here in woe and want, if he were aware of my condition."

"Why don't you write again?"

"It is useless."

"Let me write, mother. I will call him dear grandfather, and I am sure he will send you some money then: perhaps he will send for us to go to Liverpool, and live in his great house, and have servants to wait upon us."

" Alas, my child, I have given up all hope of ever seeing him again in this world. In my letters I confessed my fault, and begged his forgiveness. He cannot be alive, or I am sure my last letters would have melted his heart."

" Haven't you any brothers and sisters, mother? "

" I had one sister; and I have written several letters to her, but with no better success. They may be all dead. I fear they are."

" And your mother? "

" She died when I was young. I know Jane would have answered my letters if she had received them."

" She was your sister."

" Yes; she must be dead; and I suppose my father's property must be in the hands of strangers, covering their floors with soft carpets, and their tables with nice food, while I lie here in misery, and my poor child actually suffers from hunger;" and the afflicted mother clasped her daughter in her arms, and wept as though her heart would burst.

"Don't cry, mother. I was not very hungry. We have had enough to eat to-day. I am going to take care of you now, you have taken care of me so long," replied Katy, as she wiped away the tears that flowed down her mother's wan cheek.

"What can you do, poor child?"

"I can do a great many things; I am sure I can earn money enough to support us both."

"It is hard to think how much I have suffered, and how much of woe there may be in the future for me," sobbed Mrs. Redburn.

"Don't cry, mother. You know what it says on the watch—'ALL FOR THE BEST.' Who knows but that all your sorrows are for the best?"

"I hope they are; I will try to think they are. But it is time for you to go. Pawn the watch for as much as you can; and I trust that some fortunate event will enable us to redeem it."

Katy took the watch, smoothed down her hair again, put on her worn-out bonnet, and left the house.

CHAPTER III.

KATY AND MASTER SIMON SNEED VISIT THE PAWN-BROKER'S SHOP.

THE court in which Katy lived had once been the abode of many very respectable families, to use a popular word, for respectable does not always mean worthy of respect on account of one's virtues, but worthy of respect on account of one's lands, houses, and money. In the former sense it was still occupied by very respectable families, though none of them possessed much of the "goods that perish in the using." Mrs. Redburn, the seamstress, was very respectable; Mrs. Colvin, the washerwoman, was very respectable; so were Mrs. Howard, the tailoress, Mr. Brown, the lumper, and Mr. Sneed, the mason.

Katy's mother lived in a small house, with three

other families.   She occupied two rooms, for which she paid four dollars a month, the amount of rent now due and unpaid.   Dr. Flynch took a great deal of pleasure in telling Mrs. Redburn how his humanity and his regard for the welfare of the poor had induced him to fix the rent at so cheap a rate; but he always finished by assuring her that this sum must be promptly paid, and that no excuses could ever have any weight.

The next house to Mrs. Redburn was tenanted by Mr. Sneed, the mason.   I don't know whether I ought to say that Mr. Sneed had a son, or that Master Simon Sneed had a father, being at a loss to determine which was the more important personage of the two; but I am not going to say anything against either of them, for the father was a very honest mason, and the son was a very nice young man.

Katy knocked at the door of this house, and inquired for Master Simon Sneed.   She was informed that he had not yet finished his dinner; and she decided to wait in the court till he made his appearance.   Seating herself on the door stone, she permitted her mind to wander back to the narrative her mother had related to her.   She glanced at her coarse clothes, and could hardly believe that her grandfather was a rich merchant, and lived in a fine house.   How nice it would be if she could only find the old gentleman!   He could not be cross to her; he would give her all the money she could spend, and make a great lady of her.

"Pooh! what a fool I am to think of such a thing!" exclaimed she, impatiently, as she rose from the door stone.   "I am a beggar, and what right have I to think of being a fine lady, while my poor sick mother has nothing to eat and drink?   It is very hard to be so poor, but I suppose it is all for the best."

"Do you want me, Katy?" said a voice from the door, which Katy recognized as that of Master Simon Sneed.

"I want to see you very much," replied Katy.

"Wait a moment, and I will join you."

And in a moment Master Simon Sneed did join her; but he is so much of a curiosity, and so much of a character, that I must stop to tell my young readers all about him.

Master Simon Sneed was about fifteen years old, and tall enough to have been two years older. He was very slim, and held his head up very straight. In 1843, the period of which I write, it was the fashion for gentlemen to wear straps upon their pantaloons; and accordingly Master Simon Sneed wore straps on his pantaloons, though, it is true, the boys in the streets used to laugh and hoot at him for doing so; but they were very ill-mannered boys, and could not appreciate the dignity of him they insulted.

Master Sneed's garments were not of the finest materials, and though he was a juvenile dandy, it was evident that it required a great deal of personal labor to make him such. Clearly those straps were sewed on by himself, and clearly those cowhide shoes had been thus elaborately polished by no other hands than his own.   In a word, the appearance of his clothes, coarse as was their texture, and unfashionable as was their cut, indicated the most scrupulous care.   It was plain that he had a fondness for dress, which his circumstances did not permit him to indulge to any very great extent.

Master Simon Sneed was a great man in his own estimation; and, as he had read a great many exciting novels, and had a good command of language, he talked and acted like a great man.   He could hold his own in conversation with older and wiser persons than himself.   He could astonish almost any person of moderate pretensions by the largeness of his ideas; and, of late years, his father had not pretended to hold an argument with him, for Simon always overwhelmed him by the force and elegance of his rhetoric.   He spoke familiarly of great men and great events.

His business relations—for Master Sneed was a business man—were not very complicated.   Ac-

cording to his own reckoning, he was the chief person in the employ of Messrs. Sands & Co., wholesale and retail dry goods, Washington Street; one
who had rendered immense service to the firm, and
one without whom the firm could not possibly get
along a single day; in short, a sort of Atlas, on
whose broad shoulders the vast world of the Messrs.
Sands & Co.'s affairs rested.　But according to the
reckoning of the firm, and the general understand-
ing of people, Master Simon was a boy in the store,
whose duty it was to make fires, sweep out, and
carry bundles, and, in consideration of the fact that
he boarded himself, to receive two dollars and a
half a week for his services.　There was a vast difference between Master Simon Sneed's estimate of
Master Simon Sneed, and the Messrs. Sands &
Co.'s idea of Master Simon Sneed.

But I beg my young friends not to let anything
I have written create a prejudice against him, for
he was really a very kind-hearted young man, and
under certain circumstances would have gone a

great way to oblige a friend. He had always been exceedingly well disposed toward Katy; perhaps it was because the simple-hearted little girl used to be so much astonished when he told her about his mercantile relations with the firm of Sands & Co.; how he managed all their business for them after the store was closed at night and before the front door was unlocked in the morning; how he went to the bank after immense sums of money; and how the firm would have to give up business if he should die, or be obliged to leave them. Katy believed that Master Simon was a great man, and she wondered how his long, slim arms could accomplish so much labor, and how his small head could hold such a heap of magnificent ideas. But Master Simon, notwithstanding his elevated position in the firm, was condescending to her; he had more than once done her a favor, and had always expressed a lively interest in her welfare. Therefore she did not scruple to apply to him in the present emergency.

" Well, Katy, in what manner can I serve you? " inquired Simon, as he elevated his head, and stood picking his teeth before her.

" I want you to do something for me very much indeed."

" State your business, Katy."

" Dr. Flynch has been to our house to-day, and wants the rent; mother hasn't any money——"

" And you wish me to lend you the amount? " continued Simon, when Katy hesitated to reveal the family trouble. " It is really unfortunate, Katy; it is after bank hours now, and I don't see that I can accommodate you."

" Oh, I don't want to borrow the money."

" Ah, you don't."

" I have got a watch here, which belonged to my father; and I want to pawn it for the money to pay the rent."

" Well, it is rather out of our line of business to lend money on collateral."

" I don't want you to lend it. I want to take it

to the pawnbroker's.   Mother says I am so young and so small that they might cheat me; and I thought perhaps, maybe, you'd be so kind as to go with me."

" Go with you! " exclaimed Master Simon, as he eyed her coarse, ill-made garments.

" I thought you would," replied Katy, with a look of disappointment.

" Well, Katy, I shall be very glad to assist you in this matter, but——"

Master Simon paused, and glanced again at the unfashionable dress of the suppliant.   He was, as he said, willing to aid her; but the idea of the principal personage of the house of Sands & Co. walking through the streets of the great city with such an ill-dressed young lady was absurd, and not to be tolerated.   Master Sneed reflected.   It is undoubtedly true that " where there is a will there is a way."

" Where do you wish to go? " demanded he.

" I don't know."

"Do you know where Brattle Street is?"

"I don't, but I can find it."

"Very well; important business in another street requires my personal attention for a moment, but I will join you in Brattle Street in a quarter of an hour, and attend you to a pawnbroker's."

"Thank you."

Master Sneed gave her directions so that she could find the street, and at the end of the court, as she turned one way, he turned the other.

Katy was first at the appointed place of meeting, where Simon soon joined her; and directing her to follow him, he led the way into another street, and entered a shop.

"This young person wishes to raise some money on a watch," said Simon, as he directed the attention of the astonished broker to Katy, who was scarcely tall enough to be seen over the high counter.

"Let me see it."

Katy handed up the watch, which the money

lender opened and carefully examined. His practiced eye soon discovered that the works of the
watch were of the best quality.

" Where did you get this? " asked the broker.

" My mother gave it to me;" and Katy told without reserve the pitiful story of want and destitution
which compelled Mrs. Redburn to part with the
cherished memento of the past.

" I will give you three dollars for the watch,"
added the broker.

" Come, come, sir," interposed Master Simon,
with a smile; " that is a little too bad. A gentleman of your judgment and discretion has already
assured himself that the article is worth at least
twenty."

The broker drew a long breath after this speech,
and seemed very much impressed by the style of the
remark. But Katy declared she did not want to
sell the watch, only to pawn it.

" Your story is not a very plausible one," said
the broker, " and there is some risk in taking it."

" I give you my personal assurance, on honor, that her story is all true," added Simon.

The broker burst out into a loud laugh. He could not stand Simon's fine speeches, and would not take the watch at any rate; so they departed to find another place, and entered a shop close by.

" Where did you get this? " asked the broker, sourly; and Katy repeated her story, and Simon vouched for its truth.

" It's a lie! " cried the broker. " I will put the watch into my safe, and hand it over to the police."

" This is a most extraordinary proceeding," protested Master Simon.

" Get out of the shop, both of you, or I will hand you over to the police! You stole the watch, and have the audacity to bring it into the shop of an honest man. I don't buy stolen goods."

Katy began to cry, as the last hope of redemption from the fangs of Dr. Flynch fled. Even Master Simon Sneed was alarmed at the idea of being handed over to the police; but his sense of dignity compelled him to enter his earnest protest against the proceeding of the broker, and even to threaten him with the terrors of the law. The money lender repeated his menace, and even went to the door, for the apparent purpose of putting it in execution.

" Come, Katy, let us go; but I assure you I will represent this outrage to my friend the mayor, in such a manner that entire justice shall be done you," whispered Simon. " I cannot remain any longer away from my business, or I would recover the watch at once."

" Oh, dear! my poor mother! " sobbed Katy.

" Don't cry, my child; leave it all to me, and run home as fast as you can. You shall have the watch again, for I will call in the whole police force of Boston to your aid;" and Master Simon ran away to attend to the affairs of Sands & Co., which Katy innocently concluded must be suffering by this time from his absence.

Poor Katy! with a heavy heart she wandered home to tell her mother of this new misfortune.

CHAPTER IV.

KATY MATURES A MAGNIFICENT SCHEME.

"I suppose it is all for the best, mother," said Katy, when she had told her sad story of disappointment. "I can't get those words out of my head, since you have told me about my father. I feel just as though everything would come out right, if it does go very bad just now."

"I am glad you feel so, Katy," added Mrs. Redburn. "It will make you much better contented with your lot. I have suffered so much that I cannot help repining a little, though I feel that my destiny and yours is in the hands of the wise Father, who bringeth good out of evil."

Katy had not yet reached that spirit of meek submission to the will of Heaven which looks upward in the hour of trial, not doubting that the all-wise God knows best what is for the good of his children.   If she believed that misfortunes were all for the best it was only an impulse derived from the story of her father; a kind of philosophy which was very convenient for the evil day, because it permitted the sufferer to lie down and take things easily.   It was not a filial trust in the wisdom and mercy of the heavenly Father that sustained her as the clouds grew thicker and blacker around her; it was only a cold indifference, a feeling of the head rather than the heart.

But Mrs. Redburn had been reading the New Testament during Katy's absence, and a better and purer spirit pervaded her soul than when the weight of the blow first struck so heavily upon her.   She was well educated, and capable of reasoning in a just manner over her misfortunes; and those words on the watch seemed to convey a new meaning to her, as she considered them in the light of Christian revelation.   They were not the basis of a cold philosophy; they assured her of the paternal care of God. The thought strengthened and revived her, and when Katy appeared to announce a new trial, she received the intelligence with calmness, and felt more ready than ever before to leave her destiny in the hands of Heaven. For an hour she conversed with Katy on this subject, and succeeded in giving her some new views in relation to the meaning of the words she had so often repeated that afternoon.

The poor girl felt as she had never felt before. Upon her devolved the responsibility of providing for her mother. She had no other friend, and that day seemed to open a new era in her existence. She felt strong for the work before her, and resolved to lose not a single day in putting her resolution into operation. The teachings of her mother, breathing a spirit of piety and resignation, were grateful to her heart, and added new strength to her arm.

There was still food enough in the house for Katy's supper, for her mother could not eat, though she drank a cup of tea. The morning sun would shine upon them again, bringing another day of want and wretchedness; but the poor girl banished her fears, trusting for the morrow to Him who feedeth the hungry raven, and tempereth the wind to the shorn lamb.

She laid her head upon her pillow that night, not to sleep for many a weary hour, but to think of the future; not of its sorrows and treasured ills, but of the golden opportunities it would afford her to do something for her sick mother. At one o'clock the next day Dr. Flynch would come for the rent again, and her mother could not pay him. She felt assured he was cold and cruel enough to execute his wicked threat to turn them out of the house, though her mother had not been off her bed for many weeks. What could be done? They could not pay the rent; that was impossible; and she regarded it as just as impossible to melt the heart of Dr. Flynch. But long before she went to sleep she had decided what to do.

Worn out with fatigue and anxiety, she did not wake till a late hour; and her mother, who had kept a weary vigil all night, was glad to see her sleep so well, and did not arouse her. She was refreshed by her deep slumbers, and got up feeling like a new creature. She had scarcely made a fire and put on the tea-kettle, before a knock at the door startled her. Who could wish to see them in their poverty and want?—who but some evil person, coming to heap some new grief upon them. She scarcely had the courage to open the door; but when she did so, she saw the smiling face of Tommy Howard.

"Good-morning, Katy," said he, as he handed her a little basket he had brought. "Mother sent this over, and wants to know how Mrs. Redburn does to-day."

"She is about the same. What is in this basket, Tommy?"

"Oh, you know;" and he turned to run away.

"Stop a minute, Tommy," called Katy. "I want to speak to you."

"Well, what is it?"

"You haven't told anybody about it—have you?"

"About what?"

"What I told you yesterday," replied Katy, hanging her head with shame.

"What do you mean?"

"That we had nothing to eat;" and Katy blushed as though it was a crime to be hungry and have nothing to eat.

"Not a soul—catch me! that is, I hain't told nobody but mother."

"I am sorry you did, even her. My mother is very proud, if she is poor; but she wasn't always so poor as she is now, for she is the daughter of a rich merchant."

"You don't say so."

"Yes, I do, Tommy; so please don't say a word about it to anybody but your mother, and ask her not to mention it."

"Not a word, Katy; and mother won't either."

"And some time I'll tell you all about it. Thank you for what's in the basket, Tommy."

Without waiting for anything more, the noble, generous boy leaped down the stairs and passed out at the front door.

"What have you got there, Katy?" asked Mrs. Redburn, as she entered the room with the basket in her hand.

"Something Mrs. Howard sent us," she replied, as she opened the basket, and took out a plate of butter and half a dozen hot biscuits, which she carried to the bedside for her mother's inspection.

"What have you done, my child?" exclaimed the poor woman, a flush gathering on her pale cheek. "Have you told the neighbors that we have nothing to eat?"

"I couldn't help telling Tommy when I asked for the flounders yesterday; he told his mother, but no one else knows it."

"I had rather starve than beg, Katy; but I cannot compel you to do so."

" I will not beg."

" Then let us send those cakes back."

" No, mother; we must not be so proud as that.
I think that God sent us this food, through Mrs.
Howard, and it would be wicked to reject his
bounty."

" Do as you please, Katy."

" Some time we shall be able to pay her; and
that will make it all right."

Mrs. Redburn could not taste the biscuit, but
Katy ate heartily.   Her pride was not inflated by
the remembrance of brighter days.   All she **had**
was inherited from her mother.

After breakfast she put on her bonnet **and left**
the house, assuring her mother she should **be back**
by twelve o'clock.   She would not tell **her where**
she was going, but evaded her questions, **and got**
away as soon as she could.

As she passed down Washington Street **she**
stopped before the store of Sands & Co., for **she**
wanted to see Master Simon Sneed.   She did not

like to enter the store; so she waited on the side-walk for half an hour, hoping he would come out. As he did not appear, her impatience would not permit her to lose any more time, and she timidly opened the door, and inquired of the first salesman she saw if Mister Sneed was in.

"Mister Sneed!" laughed the clerk. "Here, Simon, is one of your friends. Wait upon her."

Simon, with a flushed cheek, came to the door. He was horrified at the insinuation of the salesman, and wished Katy had been on the other side of the ocean before she had come there to scandalize him by claiming his acquaintance.

"What do you want now?" he demanded, rather rudely. "Is it not enough that I am willing to help you, without your coming here to bring me into contempt with my associates?"

"I didn't think there was any harm in it. I waited outside for half an hour, and you didn't come out."

"I can't leave the affairs of this firm to attend

to every little——" and Master Simon's naturally good heart prevented him from uttering the unkind words that had been on his tongue. "I suppose you come to know about the watch. I haven't had time to call upon the mayor yet, but I will do so at dinner time."

"I only wanted to ask you if you know where Mrs. Gordon lives," replied Katy, very sad at the thought of the mischief she had done.

"She lives in Temple Street, over back of the State House. What do you want of her?"

"I want to see her. Do you suppose you can get that watch back?"

"I am certain I can. When my friend the mayor hears my story, you may depend upon it he will get the watch, or upset all the pawnbrokers' shops in the city."

"Are you acquainted with the mayor?" asked Katy, timidly, for, since the adventure of the previous day, she had entertained some slight doubts

in regard to the transcendent abilities of Master
Simon Sneed.

"Certainly I am. It was only last week that I
had a long and extremely interesting conversation
with his Honor on the sidewalk here before the
store."

Katy was satisfied, though Simon did not offer to
introduce her to his distinguished friend. How
could she help being satisfied in the face of such
astounding evidence? And Simon's declaration
was true, for whatever faults he had, he never
made up a story out of whole cloth. It was un-
deniably true that he had conversed with the mayor
for ten full minutes, at the time and place represented. Simon had been sent out to hold his
Honor's horse, while a lady with him did some shop-
ping; but his Honor preferred to hold his own
horse, and amused himself for the time listening to
the big talk of the nice young man.

After receiving more explicit directions in regard to the residence of Mrs. Gordon, Katy took

her leave of Simon. Next door to Sands & Co.'s was the store of a celebrated confectioner. In the window, with sundry sugar temples, cob houses of braided candy and stacks of cake, was a great heap of molasses candy; and as Katy paused for an instant to gaze at the profusion of sweet things, a great thought struck through her brain.

"Mother used to make molasses candy for me, and I know just how it is done," said she to herself. "What is the reason I can't make candy and sell it?"

She walked on toward School Street, up which she had been directed to turn, full of this idea. She would become a little candy merchant. She felt sure she could find purchasers enough, if her merchandise only looked clean and good. It was a great deal better than begging, and she thought her mother would consent to her making and selling the candy. What a glorious idea! If she could only make money enough to support her mother and herself, how happy she should be!

Full of enthusiasm at the idea of accomplishing such a vast project, she scarcely heeded the crowds of people that thronged the street and rudely jostled her. If she saw them at all, it was only to regard them as so many purchasers of molasses candy. With her brain almost reeling with the immensity and magnificence of her scheme, she reached Temple Street. After a little search she found the number of Mrs. Gordon's residence on a splendid house, whose grandness quite abashed her. But her courage revived as she thought of the purpose that had brought her there, and she boldly rang the bell. The door was opened by a servant man in a white jacket, of whom she inquired if Mrs. Gordon was at home.

"Mrs. Gordon is at home, but we don't trouble her at the call of a beggar," replied the well-fed servant, as he glanced at the homely apparel of Katy.

"I am not a beggar," she replied, with spirit, her cheek reddening with indignation at the charge.

" You can't see her; so go about your business."

" Who is it, Michael?" said a gentle voice within.

" Only a beggar, Miss Grace; she wants to see Mrs. Gordon," replied the man; and then a beautiful young lady came to look at her.

" I am not a beggar, ma'am; indeed I am not. I want to see Mrs. Gordon very much. Please to let me speak to her."

The sweet pleading tones of the child produced their impression on the beautiful lady, and she bade her come in. Katy entered, and Michael told her to stand in the entry while Miss Grace went up-stairs to call Mrs. Gordon.

CHAPTER V.

KATY VISITS MRS. GORDON, AND GETS RID OF DR.
FLYNCH.

KATY gazed with wonder and admiration at the
rich furniture of the house, and thought that perhaps her grandfather lived in as good style as Mrs.
Gordon, and that she might some day go to Liverpool and be an inmate of just such a palace. The
door of the sitting room was open, and she had an
opportunity to look at all the fine things it contained. She had never seen anything so luxurious
before, and I must say that she regretted the poverty of her lot, which deprived her mother and
herself of them.

All round the room hung pictures in costly
frames. Some of them were portraits; and one
which hung over the mantelpiece, directly before
her, soon attracted her attention, and made her for-

get the soft divans, the beautiful carpet, and the rich draperies of the windows. It was a portrait of a lady, and her expression was very like that of her mother—so like, that she could almost believe the picture had been painted for her mother. Yet that could not be, for the lady was young, and plump, and rosy, and wore rich laces, and a costly dress. She seemed to look down upon her from the golden frame with a smile of satisfaction. There was something roguish in her eye, as though she was on the point of bursting into a laugh at some mischief she had perpetrated. Oh, no! that could not be her mother; she had never seen her look like that. But there was something that seemed very much like her; and the more she looked at it, the more the picture fascinated her. She tried to look at something else, but the lady appeared to have fixed her gaze upon her, and, whichever way she turned, those laughing eyes followed her, and brought back her attention to the canvas again.

In vain she attempted to fasten her mind upon some of the other portraits. There was an elderly gentleman, with a full red face; but the jealous lady would not let her look at him. She turned round, and looked out of the windows at the side of the door; but the spell of the lady was upon her, and she could not resist the charm. The more she studied the portrait, the more convinced she became that it looked like her mother, though there was something about it which was as unlike her as anything could be.

"What makes you keep looking at me?" said Katy to herself, or rather to the lady on the canvas. "You needn't watch me so closely; I shall not steal anything."

The lady, however, insisted on watching her, and kept her roguish glance fixed upon her with a steadiness that began to make her feel nervous and uneasy; and she was greatly relieved when she heard footsteps on the stairs.

"Mrs. Gordon will be down in a moment," said

Miss Grace, in kind tones.   "Won't you come into this room and sit down?"

Katy thanked her, and Grace led her to a small chair directly under the mischievous-looking lady in the frame; and she felt a kind of satisfaction in being placed out of her sight.   But it seemed, even then, as she cast a furtive glance upward, that those roguish eyes were trying to peer over the picture frame, and get a look at her.

"Well, little girl, what do you wish with me?" said Mrs. Gordon, a benevolent-looking lady, apparently of more than forty years of age, who now entered the room.

The expression of her countenance was very pleasant, and though there were a few wrinkles on her brow, and she wore a lace cap, Katy came to the conclusion that the portrait had been taken for her.   She wondered if such a dignified lady could ever have been so roguish as the picture indicated.

"Please, ma'am," stammered she, rising from

her chair, " I come to see you about the house we live in."

" What is your name, child? "

" Katy Redburn, ma'am."

" In what house do you live? "

" In one of yours in Colvin Court.   Mother is a poor woman, and has been sick so much this summer that she can't pay the rent."

" I am very sorry for you, my child, but I refer you to my agent, Dr. Flynch.   I do not like to meddle with these things, as I have given him the whole care of my houses.   You will find him a very good man, and one who will be willing to consider your case.   He will extend to you all the lenity your case requires."

" We have told Dr. Flynch all about it, ma'am; and he says if the rent is not paid by one o'clock to-day, he shall turn us out of the house."

" Indeed! " exclaimed Mrs. Gordon; and Grace actually jumped out of her chair with astonishment and indignation.

"Yes, ma'am; that's just what he said," added Katy, satisfied with the impression she had produced.

"Is your mother ill now?" asked Mrs. Gordon.

"Yes, ma'am; she has not been off her bed for twelve weeks."

"What does Dr. Flynch say, my child?"

"He says my mother deceived him; that she told him a falsehood; and that she had money, when she didn't have a cent."

"It is too bad, mother!" exclaimed Grace.

"Hush, Grace; probably Dr. Flynch knows best, for he certainly would not turn a poor sick woman out of doors because she did not pay the rent. There may be, as he says, some deception about it, which he can penetrate and we cannot."

"There is no deception about it, ma'am," pleaded Katy, much disturbed by this sudden damper upon her hopes. "She has not got a single cent. She wouldn't tell a lie, and I wouldn't either."

There was something in the eloquence and earnestness of the child that deeply impressed the mind of the lady, and she could hardly resist the conclusion that her agent had, in this instance, made a mistake.   But she had great confidence in Dr. Flynch, and she was very unwilling to believe that he could be so harsh and cruel as the little girl represented.   She had heard of the tricks of the vicious poor, and while she was disposed to be very tender of a needy tenant, she must be just to her agent.

"It is now half past ten," continued Mrs. Gordon.   "You shall remain here, my child, and I will send Michael down to Colvin Court to inquire into the situation of your mother.   He must be impartial, for he knows nothing about the case."

"Thank you, ma'am," said Katy, with a promptness which assured Grace, if not her mother, that the little girl was honest.

Mrs. Gordon rang the bell, and when Michael answered the summons, she attended him to the street door, where she instructed him to call upon Mrs. Redburn, and also to inquire of the grocer at the corner, and of her neighbors, what sort of a person she was. The lady returned to the sitting room when he had gone, and asked Katy a great many questions about herself and her mother, and thus nearly an hour was consumed; at the end of which time Michael returned. Katy had answered all the lady's questions so fairly, though without betraying her family history, which her mother had cautioned her to keep to herself, that she was prepared to receive a favorable report from her man.

"Well, Michael, did you find the woman at home?" asked Mrs. Gordon, as the man presented himself.

"Indeed, I did, marm."

"What was she doing?"

"She was fast in bed, and told me she hadn't been able to leave it for twelve weeks come Saturday."

"What does the grocer say?"

"He says she is a very good woman, but poor and proud. She always paid him every cent she owed him, and he'd trust her for half he has in his shop."

"That will do, Michael; you may go;" and the man retired with a respectful bow.

Katy's face wore a smile of triumph as Michael was dismissed. Her mother's truthfulness had been vindicated, and it was the proudest moment she had known for many a day.

"How long has your mother lived in my house?" asked Mrs. Gordon.

"About three years, ma'am; and she always paid her rent till this month," replied Katy.

"If she had not, Dr. Flynch would have turned her into the street," added Grace; and it was evident the beautiful young lady had no special regard for that worthy gentleman.

"We have tried hard enough to pay the rent this month," continued Katy; and she proceeded to tell the story of the silver watch that had belonged to her father.

" This is dreadful, mother; let us do something about it," said Grace. " What a wretch the broker must have been! "

" We will endeavor to get the watch back for her," replied Mrs. Gordon, as she seated herself at a table and wrote a few lines on a piece of paper. " Here, my child, is a receipt for your month's rent. When Dr. Flynch comes for the money, you show him this, and he will be satisfied;" and she handed her the receipt.

Katy took it, and thanked the good lady, assuring her that her mother would certainly pay the money as soon as she got well.

" My mother is poor and proud, just as the grocer said, and she don't ask anyone to give her anything. I am going to earn some money myself, and I hope I shall be able to pay the next month's rent," added Katy, as she moved toward the door.

" But the watch, mother? " interposed Grace.

"If the little girl will come here this afternoon or to-morrow morning, we will take her to the mayor, who will have the case attended to."

"I will come any time, ma'am."

"The mayor is my friend, and I will call at his house with you this afternoon at about three o'clock."

Katy could not but think the mayor had a great many friends, for there was Master Simon Sneed, and Mrs. Gordon, and she knew not how many more. She thanked the lady very warmly for her kindness, and promising to come at the time stated, she took her leave. She was followed to the door by Grace, who detained her there.

"Katy, I am sure you are a very good little girl, and here is a dollar for you. It will buy something good for your mother."

"I thank you very much, Miss Gordon. I am poor, but proud, like my mother," replied she, as a flush of shame mantled her cheek.

"What a foolish little girl!" laughed Grace.

"Take it; you will oblige me **very** much by taking it."

"No, ma'am, I can't; my mother wouldn't own
me if I should take money as a gift."

"But you must take it, Katy; I shall be angry if
you don't."

The little girl looked up into her pretty eyes,
beaming with pity and love; and she could hardly
resist the temptation to oblige her by accepting the
gift; but since she had heard the story of her
mother's life, she understood why she was so much
prouder than other poor people; and as she thought
of her grandfather in his fine house in the great
city of Liverpool, she felt a little of the same spirit
—she too was poor and proud. Besides, as Grace
jingled the two half dollars together, there was a
harmony in the sound that suggested a great heap
of good things for her mother. And there was another powerful consideration that weighed with
great force upon her mind. One of those half
dollars would be a sufficient capital upon which to

commence her candy speculation. It would buy ever so much molasses of the very best quality. As she thought of this, she was disposed, at least, to compromise with Miss Grace.

"I cannot accept the money as a gift, but you may lend it to me, if you please," said Katy, after she had reflected a moment.

"Just as you like," laughed Grace; "but I shall not feel bad if you never pay me."

"I shall certainly pay it again," persisted the embryo candy merchant. "I would not take it if I thought I could not."

"Very well; but you must know I think you are a very singular little girl."

"I am poor and proud, that's all."

Katy took the loan, and with her fancy fired with brilliant expectations in regard to the candy operation, ran home to her mother as fast as her feet would carry her. Mrs. Redburn was much displeased with her at first for what she had done. Her pride revolted at the thought of begging a favor; but Katy explained the matter so well that she was satisfied, though nothing was said about the loan she had obtained.

Punctually at the appointed hour came Dr. Flynch for the rent.

"Have you got the money?" he demanded in his usual bland tones, though Katy thought she could see a wicked purpose in his little gray eye.

"No, sir; but——"

"That's all I desire to know, Mrs. Redburn," interrupted the agent. "You must leave the house."

"But, sir, I have something that will do as well as the money," added the sick woman.

"Have you, indeed?" sneered Dr. Flynch. "I think not."

"Will you read that, sir?" said Katy, handing him Mrs. Gordon's receipt.

The agent took the paper, and as he read, the wonted serenity of his brow was displaced by a dark scowl.   His threats had been disregarded, and he had been reported to his employer.

"So you have been fawning and cringing upon Mrs. Gordon," growled he.   "Probably you have told her more lies than you dared tell me."

"I told her nothing but the truth, and she sent her man down here to find out all about us," said Katy smartly.

"Very well; this paper will only delay the matter for a few days; when I have exposed you to her, she will acquiesce in my views;" and Dr. Flynch threw down the receipt and left the house.

"We are well rid of him, at any rate," said Katy.   "Now I will get you some dinner, for I must be at Mrs. Gordon's at three o'clock; and I want to tell you about my plan too, mother."

The active little girl made a cup of tea for her mother, and the dinner was soon despatched.

CHAPTER VI.

KATY PREPARES A STOCK OF MERCHANDISE.

KATY had not time then to tell her mother about the candy speculation she had in view, and she was obliged to wait till her return from Temple Street. Promptly at the hour she presented herself at Mrs. Gordon's, and they went to the house of the mayor; but that distinguished gentleman was not at home, and the lady promised to go again with her the next day.

As she walked home she thought of what she should say to her mother in favor of the candy project, for she felt sure her mother's pride would throw many obstacles in her path. The best argument she could think of was, that the business would be an honest calling and, though she was too proud to beg, she was not too proud to work or to take a very humble position among the people around her. She did not look upon the act of selling candy to the passers-by in the streets as degrading in itself, and therein she differed very widely from her mother, who had been brought up in ease and affluence. Before she got home she had made up her mind what she should say, and how she should defend her plan from the assaults of pride.

"Now, mother, you shall hear my plan," she continued, after she had announced the ill success of her visit to the mayor's house. "I am going into business, and I expect to make a great deal of money."

"Are you, indeed?" replied Mrs. Redburn, smiling at the enthusiasm of her daughter.

"I am; and you must not be angry with me, or object very much to my plan."

"Well, what is your plan?"

"I am going to sell candy," said Katy, pausing to notice the effect of this startling declaration. "You know what nice molasses candy you used to make for me.   Mrs. Sneed and Mrs. Colvin said a great many times that it was a good deal better than they could buy at the shops."

" But, child, I am not able to make candy now. I cannot get off my bed."

" I will make it; you shall lay there and tell me how.   I am sure I can make it."

" It is very hard work to pull it."

" I won't mind that."

" Suppose you can make it, how will you sell it? " asked Mrs. Redburn, casting an anxious glance at the enthusiastic little girl.

" Oh, I shall take a box, and offer it to the folks that pass along the streets."

" Are you crazy, Katy? " exclaimed the mother, raising her head on the bed.   " Do you think I could permit you to do such a thing? "

" Why not, mother? "

" What a life for a child to lead?   Do you think I could let you wander about the streets exposed to the insults and rude jests of the vicious and thoughtless? You do not understand what you propose."

" I think I do, mother.   I don't see any harm in selling candy to those who are willing to buy."

" Perhaps there is no harm in the mere act of selling candy; but what a life for you to lead!   It makes me shudder to think of it."

" It is your pride, mother."

" I am thankful I have some pride left, Katy."

" But, mother, we can't be poor and proud.   We haven't got any money to be proud with."

" I am proud, I know; I wish I could banish it," replied Mrs. Redburn, with a deep sigh.

" Let me try the plan, mother, and if I can't get along with it, I will give it up."

" It will subject you to a great many trials and temptations."

" I can manage them, mother."

" Can you submit to the insults of evil-minded persons? "

" Yes, mother; no decent person would insult me,

and I don't care for others.   I can pity them, and run away from them.   I am not afraid of anything. Do let me try."

Mrs. Redburn saw that Katy was too earnest to be thwarted; that, impelled by a noble purpose, she had set her heart upon making the attempt, and she did not like to disappoint her.   It is true, she keenly felt the degradation of such a life, and even feared that Katy might be led astray while pursuing such an occupation; but she gave a reluctant consent, trusting that one or two experiments would disgust her with the business.

Katy clapped her hands with joy as her mother's scruples gave way, and she found herself at liberty to carry her plan into execution.   It seemed to her as though she had crossed the threshold of fortune and had actually entered the great temple.   She had an opportunity to accomplish a great work, and her enthusiasm would not permit her to doubt in regard to her final success.

"I must begin now, mother, and make all the

candy this afternoon, so that I can commence sell-ing it early to-morrow morning. I will go to the grocery now and get the molasses."

"Poor child; you have nothing to get it with. We have no money; you did not think of that."

"Yes, I did, and I have the money to buy the molasses. I borrowed it," replied Katy, evincing some confusion.

"You borrowed it? Pray who would lend you money?"

"Miss Grace Gordon."

"Did you borrow it, Katy?" asked Mrs. Red-burn, casting a reproachful glance at her.

"Yes, mother, I did. I would not accept money now, after what you have said to me. Miss Grace wanted to give it to me, but I told her I could not take it. She laughed at me, and I said I was poor and proud. She would make me take it, and said so much, that, at last, I told her if she would lend it to me, I would take it."

"It was the same as a gift," said Mrs. Redburn,

blushing with shame at the thought of accepting alms.

" No, it wasn't; she may think it was, but I mean to pay her, and I shall pay her; I know I shall."

" If you can," sighed the proud mother.

" I shall be able to pay her soon, for I mean to sell lots of candy."

" You may be disappointed."

" No; I am sure I shall sell a good deal; I mean to make people buy.   I shall talk up smart to them, just as the shopkeepers do; I am going to tell them what good candy it is, and that their little sons and daughters will like it very much."

" You are beside yourself, Katy.   It pains me to hear you talk so.   It is sad to think a child of mine should relish such an employment as that in which you are going to engage."

" Do you remember the book my Sunday-school teacher gave me last New Year's day, mother?   It was all about false pride; I want you to read it, mother.   We can't afford to be so proud."

"Go and get your molasses, Katy," replied Mrs. Redburn, who could not but acknowledge the truth of her daughter's remarks.

She had read the book alluded to, and was not willing to confront the arguments it had put in the mouth of her child. She was conscious that her pride, which made a humble occupation repulsive to her, was a false pride. If it could have been carried on in private, it would not have seemed so galling. For years she had been a recluse from society, mingling only with her humble neighbors, and with them no more than her circumstances required. She had labored in solitude, and shunned observation as much as possible, by carrying her work back and forth in the evening. Years of hard toil had not familiarized her with the circumstances of her lot. She tried to be humble and submissive, but the memory of her early days could not be driven away.

Katy returned in a few minutes with the jug of molasses. She bustled round and made up a good fire, got the kettle on, and everything in readiness for the work. Her mother gave her directions how to proceed; but Katy could impart to her none of her own enthusiasm.

When the molasses had been cooked enough, she was ready to commence the pulling, which was the most difficult part in the manufacture of her merchandise. Then she found that her trials had indeed commenced. At first the sticky mass, in spite of the butter and the flour with which she had plentifully daubed her hands, was as obstinate as a mule. It would not work one way or another; now it melted down, and stuck to her fingers, and then it became as solid as a rock. She fretted some at these crosses, and as her spirits sank her mother's rose, for she thought Katy's resolution would not hold out long enough for her to complete the experiment. But she underrated the energy of the devoted girl, who in the face of every discouragement, stuck to the candy with as much zeal as the candy stuck to her.

As is almost always the case with those who per-severe to the end, Katy soon won a partial triumph, which gladdened her heart, and gave her courage to continue her trying labors. She had worked a portion of the mass into candy—clear, light-colored, inviting candy. Columbus felt no prouder of his achievement when he had crossed the Atlantic, or Napoleon when he had passed the Alps. She danced for joy as she gazed upon the clear, straight sticks of candy, as they were ar-ranged in the pan. It was a great conquest for her; but at what a sacrifice it had been won! Her little hands, unused to such hard work, were blis-tered in a dozen places, and smarted as though they had been scalded with boiling water. She showed them to her mother, who begged her not to do any more; but she had too much enthusiasm to be deterred by the smart of her wounds, and reso-lutely resumed her labor.

She had scarcely commenced upon the second mass before her operations were interrupted by the entrance of Mrs. Howard, her friend Tommy's mother.

"Why, what are you doing, child?" asked the good woman. "I thought you were all sick, and here you are making candy, as merry as on a feast day."

"I am making it to sell, Mrs. Howard," replied Katy proudly.

"Bless me! but you're a queer child! Do you think folks will buy it of you?"

"I know they will;" and Katy detailed her plan to the interested neighbor, declaring she was sure she could support her mother and herself by making and selling candy. "But is is hard work," she added; "see how I've blistered my hands."

"Poor child! it's enough to kill you!" exclaimed Mrs. Howard, as she glanced at the great blisters on Katy's hands.

"I have been trying to make her give up the idea, but she has more courage than I ever gave her credit for," remarked Mrs. Redburn.

"It's a shame for you to hurt your hands in this manner; but I daresay they will soon get hard, like mine, with the labor," replied Mrs. Howard, as she threw off her hood and rolled up her sleeves. "Here, child, let me help you."

"You are very kind, ma'am; and I hope I shall be able to do something for you some time."

"Never you mind that; you are a nice girl, and it does my heart good to see you trying to help your mother," added the kind woman, as she detached a large mass of candy, and commenced pulling it with a vigor that astonished the weak-handed little girl. "You're a jewel and a blessing, and you're worth a dozen of the fine ladies that are too proud to lift a finger to keep their bodies from starving. Ah, it's a dreadful misfortune to be proud."

"To be poor and proud," said Mrs. Redburn.

"You are right, ma'am; and I am glad to see you have none of it here; for some of your neighbors used to say you were too proud to speak to them."

Mrs. Redburn made no reply, and permitted her kind neighbor, whose tongue scarcely ceased to swing for a moment, to continue her remarks without opposition. She and Katy worked with all their might till the candy was ready for market, and when the poor invalid poured out her thanks she ran off and left them.

The exultation with which Katy regarded her plentiful stock of merchandise almost caused her to forget her smarting hands; and when she could no longer keep her eyes open, she went to sleep to dream of great operations in molasses candy on 'change next day.

CHAPTER VII.

KATY MAKES A LARGE SALE.

KATY rose the next morning bright and early, and her heart was full of hope. She felt that she had a great work to perform, and she was going forth to do it, resolved that no obstacle should turn her back. Her mother had told her that she would be laughed at, and made fun of; that thoughtless people would look down upon her with contempt, and that wicked ones would insult her. She was, therefore, prepared for all these trials, but she had braced herself up to meet them with courage and fortitude.

Her mother was sick, and they were actually in a suffering condition. What right had she to be proud in her poverty? She felt able to support her mother, and she could find no excuse, if she wished to do so, for not supporting her. It was her duty, therefore, to sell candy, if she could get money by it; and this consideration strengthened her heart.

Katy had been to the public school and to the Sunday school until her mother was taken sick; and though she was only eleven years old, she had a very good idea of her moral and religious duties. "Honor thy father and thy mother," the commandment says; and she could think of no better way to obey the Divine precept than to support her mother when there was no one else upon whom she could rely. Little by little their earthly possessions had passed away. Mrs. Redburn had never learned how to save money; and when the day of adversity came, her funds were soon exhausted. She had no friends to whom she dared reveal her poverty, and when want came to the door, she was too proud to beg. Hoping for better days, she had sold most of her best dresses, and those of Katy. The small sums raised by these sacrifices were soon used up; and when the daughter could no longer make a decent appearance, she was required to show herself much more than ever before. Katy did not repine at this, though her mother did, for their pride, as my young friends have discovered, was of very different kinds.

Katy did wish she had a little better dress, and a little better bonnet for her first attempt in the mercantile calling; but there was no help for it. She had mended her clothes as well as she could, and as they were clean, she was pretty well satisfied with her personal appearance. Besides, people would not be half so apt to buy her candy if she were well dressed, as if she were rather plainly clothed. In short, it was all for the best.

After breakfast she prepared herself for the duties of the day. Her heart beat violently with anxiety and expectation, and while she was placing the candy on the tray, which she had previously covered with white paper, to render her wares the more inviting, her mother gave her a long lecture on the trials and difficulties in her path, and the proper way to encounter them.

"Now, my dear child," said Mrs. Redburn, in conclusion, "if any evil person insults you, do not resent it, but run away as fast as you can."

"Shan't I say anything, mother?"

"Not a word."

"But if some naughty boy or girl, no bigger than I am myself, should be saucy to me, I think I can give them as good as they send."

"Don't do it, Katy."

"They have no business to insult me."

"That is very true; but when you use bad or violent language to them, you go down to their level."

"But if they begin it?"

"No matter, Katy; if they are unkind and wicked, it is no reason that you should be unkind and wicked. If you leave them without resenting their insults, the chances are that they will be ashamed of themselves before you get out of sight. You need not be low and vile because others are."

"I guess you are right, mother."

"You know what the Bible says; 'If thine enemy hunger, feed him; if he thirst, give him drink; for in so doing thou shalt heap coals of fire on his head.'"

"I won't say a word, mother, whatever they say to me. I'll be as meek as Moses."

"I hope you will not be gone long," added Mrs. Redburn.

"I have thirty sticks of candy here. I don't think it will take me long to sell the whole of them. I shall be back by dinner time, whether I sell them or not, for you know I must go to Mrs. Gordon again to-day. Now, good-by, mother; and don't you worry about me, for I will do everything just as though you were looking at me."

Katy closed the door behind her, and did not see the great tears that slid down her mother's pale cheek as she departed. It was well she did not, for it would have made her heart very sad to know all the sorrow and anxiety that distressed her mother as she saw her going out into the crowded streets of a great city, to expose herself to a thousand temptations. She wept long and bitterly in the solitude of her chamber; and perhaps her wounded pride caused many of her tears to flow. But better thoughts came at last, and she took up the Bible which lay on the bed, and read a few passages. Then she prayed to God that he would be with Katy in the midst of the crowd, and guide her safely through the perils and temptations that would assail her. She tried to banish her foolish pride; when she considered her circumstances she could almost believe it was a wicked pride; but when she endeavored to be reconciled to her lot, the thought of her father's fine house, and the servants that used to wait upon her, came up, and the struggle in her heart was very severe. In spite of all she had said to Katy about the disgrace of selling candy in the streets, she could not but be thankful that the poor girl had none of her foolish pride. She read in the New Testament about the lowly life which Jesus and the apostles led, and then asked herself what right she had to be proud.   And thus she struggled through the long hours she remained alone—trying to be humble, trying to be good and true.   Those who labor and struggle as hard as she did are always the better for it, even though they do not achieve a perfect triumph over the passions that torment them.

Katy blushed when she met the keeper of the grocery at the corner of the court, for in spite of all her fine talk about false pride, she had not entirely banished it from her heart.   Some queer ideas came into her head as she thought what she was doing.   What would her grandfather, the rich Liverpool merchant, say, should he meet her then! Of course he would not know her; he would be ashamed of her.   But she did not permit such reflections as these to influence her; and as soon as she was conscious of the nature of her thoughts she banished them.

" I'm going to support my mother, and I have no right to be proud.   If I meet my grandfather, I should very much like to sell him twenty sticks of candy."

"Hallo, Katy!　What are you going to do?" said a voice behind, which she recognized as that of her friend Tommy Howard.

"I'm going to sell this molasses candy," replied Katy.

"You're a spunky one; mother told me all about it.　I should like two sticks," said Tommy, as he offered her the money.

"Take two, Tommy, and as many more as you like."

"Two is all I want;" and he placed the two cents on the tray.

"No, Tommy, I won't take your money," replied Katy, with a blush, for she felt ashamed to take his money.

"That's no way to trade," laughed Tommy. "You won't make much, if you do so.　Keep the money and I will keep the candy."

"I can't keep it, Tommy."

" You must; if you don't take the money, I won't take the candy."

" I owe you two cents, Tommy.   I will pay you now."

" No, you don't! "

" Please to take them; I shall feel very bad, if you don't."

Tommy Howard looked her in the eye a moment; he saw a tear there.   Her pride was wounded, and he took the two cents from the tray, for he did not wish to give her pain.

" Now we are square, Tommy," said Katy, as her face brightened up again.

" Yes, we are, but I don't like it pretty well. One of these days, when you get out of this scrape, I will let you give me as much candy as you have a mind to."

This was very obliging of Tommy; and when Katy understood his motive, she was sorry she had not permitted him to pay for the candy, for she saw that he did not feel just right about the transaction.   It was not exactly mercantile, but then the heart comes before commerce.   As she walked along, she could not help thinking that her natural generosity might seriously interfere with the profits of her enterprise.   She had a great many friends, and it became a knotty question for her to decide whether, if she met any of her school companions, she should give each of them a stick of candy.   She would like to. do so very much indeed, but it was certain she could not afford to pursue such a liberal policy.   It was a hard question, and, hoping she should not meet any of her schoolmates, she determined to refer it to her mother for settlement.

When she got into Washington Street she felt that the time for action had come.   Now was the time to sell candy; and yet she did not feel like asking folks to buy her wares.   The night before, as she lay thinking about her business, it had all seemed very easy to her; but now it was quite a different thing.   No one seemed to take any notice of her, or to feel the least interest in the great mission she had undertaken. But Katy was aware that it requires some effort in these days to sell goods, and she must work; she must ask people to buy her candy.

There was a nice-looking gentleman, with a good-natured face, coming down the street, and she resolved to make a beginning with him. He couldn't say much more than No to her, and she placed herself in a position to accost him. But when he came near enough, her courage all oozed out, and she let him pass without speaking to him.

"What a fool I am!" exclaimed she to herself, when he had passed. "I shall never do anything in this way. There comes another gentleman who looks as though he had a sweet tooth; at any rate, he seems as good-natured as a pound of sugar. I will certainly try him."

Her heart pounded against her ribs as though it had been worked by a forty-horse engine—poor girl. It was a great undertaking to her; quite as great as taking a six-story granite warehouse, piling it full of merchandise from cellar to attic, and announcing himself as ready for business, to a child of a larger growth. Everything seemed to hang on the issues of that tremendous moment.

" Buy some candy? " said she, in tremulous tones, her great, swelling heart almost choking her utterance.

" No, child. I don't want any," replied the gentleman kindly, as he glanced at the tray on which the candy had been so invitingly spread.

" It is very nice," stammered Katy; " and perhaps your children at home would like some, if you do not."

Bravo, Katy! That was very well done, though the gentleman was an old bachelor, and could not appreciate the full force of your argument.

" Are you sure it is very nice? " asked the gentleman, with a benevolent smile, when he had laughed heartily at Katy's jumping conclusion.

" I know it is," replied the little candy merchant, very positively.

"Then you may give me six sticks;" and he threw a fourpence on her tray.

Six sticks! Katy was astounded at the magnitude of her first commercial transaction. Visions of wealth, a fine house, and silk dresses for her mother and herself, danced through her excited brain, and she thought that her grandfather, the great Liverpool merchant, would not have been ashamed of her, if he had been present to witness that magnificent operation.

"Have you any paper to wrap it up in?" asked the gentleman.

Here was an emergency for which Katy had not provided. Her grandest expectations had not extended beyond the sale of one stick at a time, and she was not prepared for such a rush of trade. However, she tore off a piece from one of the white sheets at the bottom of the tray, wrapped up the six sticks as nicely as she could, and handed them to the gentleman, who then left her awaiting another customer.

Katy, elated by her first success, ran home as fast as she could to procure some more white paper, of which she had a dozen sheets that had been given to her by a friend. It was in the back room, so that she did not disturb her mother, choosing to astonish her with the whole story of her success at noon.

CHAPTER VIII.

KATY SELLS OUT, AND VISITS THE MAYOR.

KATY reached Washington Street once more. She had lost all her timidity, and would not have feared to accost the governor, if she had met him and request him to purchase a cent's worth of mc lasses candy.

"Buy some candy?" said she to the first person who passed near her.

"No!" was the prompt and emphatic answer of the gentleman addressed.

"It is very nice," suggested Katy.

"Get out of my way," growled the gentleman, and the little candy merchant deemed it prudent to heed the command.

She was nettled by this rude reception, and would have been disposed to resent it, if there had been any way for her to do so.   She had not yet learned to bear up against the misfortunes of trade, and her eye followed the sour gentleman far down the street.   Why should he treat her in such a rude and unkind manner?   What would he say if she should tell him that her grandfather was a great Liverpool merchant, lived in a big house, and had lots of servants to wait upon him?   She was as good as he was, any day.

" Give me a stick of candy," said a nice little girl with a silk dress on, whom a lady was holding by the hand, at the same time placing a cent on her tray.

Katy started at the words, and reproved herself for her want of meekness.   She might, perhaps, have sold half a dozen sticks of candy while she had been watching the sour gentleman, and persuading herself that she had been very badly used. She tore off a piece of paper, in which she wrapped up the candy for the purchaser, and handed it to her.

"Thank you," said she, as she picked up the copper, and transferred it to her pocket.

"Your candy looks very nice," added the lady, evidently pleased with Katy's polite manners.

"It's very nice, ma'am."

"Have you sold much to-day?"

"No, ma'am; I have but just come out."

"It looks so good, I will take half a dozen sticks for the children at home."

"Thank you, ma'am; you are very kind," replied Katy; and she soon made a nice little parcel for the lady, who gave her a fourpence.

Here was another avalanche of good fortune, and the little candy merchant could hardly believe her senses.   At this rate she would soon become a wholesale dealer in the article.

"Buy some candy?" said she, addressing the next person she met.

"No."

"Buy some candy?" she continued, turning to the next.

" No."

And so she went from one to another, and no one seemed to have the least relish for molasses candy. She walked till she came to State Street, and sold only three sticks.   She had begun to be a little disheartened, for the success she had met with at the beginning had raised her anticipations so high that she was not disposed to be content with moderate sales.   While she was standing at the corner of State Street, waiting impatiently for customers, she saw a man with a basket of apples enter a store.   She crossed the street to observe what he did in the store, in order, if possible, to get an idea of his mode of doing business.   She saw him offer his apples to the clerks and others in the shop, and she was surprised and gratified to see that nearly every person purchased one or more of them.   In her heart she thanked the apple man for the hint he had unconsciously afforded her, and resolved to profit by his example.

Now that commerce was her business, she was

disposed to make it her study; and as she reasoned over the matter, she came to understand why she found so few buyers in the street. Ladies and gentlemen did not like to be seen eating candy in the street; neither would many of them want to put it into their pockets, where it would melt and stick to their clothes. They would eat it in their shops and houses; and with this new idea she was encouraged to make a new effort. Walking along till she came to a store where there appeared to be several clerks, she entered.

"Buy some candy?" said she, addressing a salesman near the window, as she raised up her wares so that he could see them.

The clerk made no reply, but coming round from behind the counter, he rudely took her arm, opened the door, and pushed her into the street. Katy's cheek burned with indignation at this unprovoked assault, and she wished for the power of ten men, that she might punish the ill-natured fellow as he deserved. But it was all for the best, for, in push-

ing her out of the shop, the clerk threw her against
a portly gentleman on the street, whose soft, yield-
ing form alone saved her from being tumbled into
the gutter.   He showed no disposition to resent the
assault upon his obesity, and kindly caught her in
his arms.

"What is the matter, my dear?" said the gentleman, in soothing tones.

"That man pushed me out of the store," replied
Katy, bursting into tears, for she was completely
overcome by the indignity that had been cast upon
her.

"Perhaps you didn't behave well."

"I am sure I did. I only asked him to buy
some candy; and he shoved me right out the door,
just as though I had been a dog."

"Well, well, don't cry, my dear; you seem to be
a very well-behaved little girl, and I wonder at finding you in such a low business."

"My mother is sick, and I am trying to earn
something to support her," sobbed Katy, who, with

her independent notions of trade in general, and of the candy trade in particular, would not have revealed this humiliating truth, except under the severe pressure of a wounded spirit.

" Poor child! " exclaimed the portly gentleman, thrusting his hand deep down into his pocket, and pulling up a handful of silver. " Here is half a dollar for you, for I know you tell the truth."

" Oh, no, sir; I can't take money as a gift."

" Eh ? "

The gentleman looked astonished, and attempted to persuade her; but she steadily protested against receiving his money as a gift.

" You are a proud little girl, my dear."

" I am poor and proud; but I will sell you some candy."

" Well, give me half a dollar's worth."

" I haven't got so much. I have only fourteen cents' worth left."

" Give me that, then."

Katy wrapped up the remainder of her stock in a

piece of paper, and handed it to the gentleman, who in payment threw the half dollar on the tray.

" I can't change it."

" Never mind the change;" and the fat gentleman hurried away.

Katy was so utterly astounded to find she had disposed of her entire stock, that she did not have the presence of mind to follow him, and the half dollar had to be placed in her treasury. She did not regard it with so much pride and pleasure as she did the two fourpences and the four coppers, for there was something unmercantile about the manner in which it had come into her possession. She could not feel satisfied with herself, as she walked toward home, till she had argued the matter, and effected a compromise between her pride and her poverty. She had sold candy for the money, and the gentleman had paid her over three cents a stick—rather above the market value of the article; but there was no other way to make the transaction correspond with her ideas of propriety.

Her work was done for the forenoon, though she had plenty of candy at home. It was now eleven o'clock, and she had not time to sell out another stock before dinner. As she walked up the street, on her way home, she encountered Master Simon Sneed, who, with the dignity and stateliness of a merchant prince, was lugging a huge bundle of goods to the residence of some customer.

"I am glad to see you, Simon," said Katy. "Have you seen your friend the mayor?"

"I am sorry to inform you, Katy, that a press of business has prevented my calling on his Honor."

"I am sorry for that. I am afraid I shall never see the watch again."

"Depend upon it, you shall. I pledge you my honor that I will use every exertion to recover the lost treasure. Just now our firm require the undivided attention of all in the store."

"I told Mrs. Gordon all about it, and she promised to speak to the mayor."

"It was unnecessary to trouble her with the matter; my influence with the mayor will be quite sufficient."

"I dare say it will; but when shall you see him?"

"Very soon; be patient, Katy."

"Mrs. Gordon promised to take me to the mayor to-day, and tell him all about it."

"Take *you* to the mayor!" exclaimed Master Simon.

"That's what she said."

"You will be afraid of him, and not able to tell your story."

"No, I guess I shan't. I will tell him that I have mentioned the matter to you."

"Perhaps you had better not; his Honor, though we have been quite intimate, may not remember my name. But I must leave you now, for the firm get very uneasy in my absence."

Simon shouldered his bundle again, and moved off, and Katy walked toward home, wondering why a person of so much importance to the Messrs.

Sands & Co. should be permitted to degrade himself by carrying bundles. When she got home she found her mother in a very cheerful frame of mind, the result of her reading and meditation.

"Well, Katy, you come back with an empty tray; have you sold all your candy?" asked Mrs. Redburn, as she entered the room.

"Yes, mother, every stick. I have brought back sixty-six cents," replied Katy, emptying her pocket on the bed.

"Sixty-six cents! But you had only thirty sticks of candy."

"You must not blame me for what I have done, mother; I could not help it;" and she proceeded to narrate all the particulars of her forenoon's occupation.

Mrs. Redburn was annoyed at the incident with the fat gentleman; more so than by the rudeness to which Katy had been subjected. The little merchant was so elated at her success that her mother could not find it in her heart to cast a damper upon her spirits by a single reproach. Perhaps her morning's reflections had subdued her pride so that she did not feel disposed to do so.

After dinner Katy hastened at once to Temple Street again. To her great disappointment she found that Mrs. Gordon and her daughter had been suddenly called to Baltimore by the death of one of her husband's near relatives. But the kind lady had not forgotten her, and that was a great consolation. Michael gave her a note, directed to the mayor, which he instructed her to deliver that day.

With the assistance of Michael she found the house of the mayor, and though her heart beat violently, she resolutely rang the bell at the door.

" Is the mayor in? " asked she of the sleek servant man that answered the summons.

" Well, suppose he is; what of it? " replied the servant, who could not possibly have been aware that Katy's grandfather was a rich Liverpool merchant, or he would have spoken more civilly to her.

" I want to see him."

"He don't see little brats like you," answered the servant, shutting the door in her face.

Katy was indignant. She wished a dozen things all at once; and among other things, she wished Master Simon Sneed had been there, that he might report the circumstance to his friend the mayor. What was to be done? It was mean to treat her in that shabby manner, and she would not stand it! She would not, that she wouldn't! Grasping the bell handle with a courageous hand, she gave a pull that must have astonished the occupants of the servants' hall, and led them to believe that some distinguished character had certainly come. The sleek man servant reappeared at the door, ready to make his lowest bow to the great personage, when he beheld the flashing eye of Katy.

"How dare you ring that bell again?" snarled he.

"I want to see the mayor; I have a note for him from Mrs. Gordon, and I won't go away till I see him."

" From Mrs. Gordon!   Why didn't you say so?
You may come in."

Katy entered at this invitation, and the man bade
her wait in the hall till he informed the mayor of
her errand.   She was not a little pleased with the
victory she had gained, and felt quite equal,
after it, to the feat of facing the chief magistrate
of the city.   While she stood there, a little boy,
having in his hand a stick of molasses candy, with
which he had contrived plentifully to bedaub his
face, came out of the adjoining room, and surveyed
her carefully from head to foot.   Katy looked at
the candy with attention, for it looked just like one
of the sticks she had sold that forenoon.   The little
fellow, who was not more than five or six years of
age, seemed to have a hearty relish for the article,
and as he turned it over, Katy assured herself that
it was a portion of her stock.

" My pa brought home lots of candy," said the
little fellow, after he had satisfied himself with the
survey of Katy's person.

" Do you like it? " asked she, willing to cultivate his acquaintance.

" Don't I, though! "

" Where did your father get it? "

" He bought it of a little girl; she was poor and proud," replied the little gentleman, transferring half an inch of the candy to his mouth.

" Dear me! " exclaimed Katy.

But her conversation was interrupted by the return of the servant, who directed Katy to follow him upstairs.

CHAPTER IX.

KATY TALKS WITH THE MAYOR, AND RECOVERS THE WATCH.

KATY followed the servant man, whose name was John, upstairs; but at the first turn he stopped, and begged her not to mention that he had shut the door upon her.

"I don't know," said Katy. "I gave you no reason to treat me in that ugly manner."

"You didn't; but, you see, I thought you was some beggar, coming to disturb his Honor."

"Do I look like a beggar?" asked Katy.

"Indeed you don't; that was a bad blunder of mine. If you mention it, I shall lose my place."

"Well, I won't say a word then; but I hope you will learn better manners next time."

"Thank you, miss; and be sure I'll treat you like a lady next time."

John then conducted her upstairs into a room, the walls of which were almost covered with books. Katy thought what a wise man the mayor must be, for she had never seen so many books before in her life, and took it for granted the mayor had read them all. As she entered the apartment she saw a fat gentleman sitting at the desk, very busy in examining a great pile of papers. When he turned his head, Katy was not much surprised to see that it was the nice gentleman who had given her half a dollar for fourteen cents' worth of candy.

"Ah, my dear, it is you!" exclaimed the mayor, smiling pleasantly, as he recognized the little candy merchant.

"Yes, sir; if you please, it is me," stammered Katy, making her obeisance, and feeling very much confused, for it was the first time she had ever come into the presence of a great man, and she could not exactly tell whether she ought to get down on her knees, as she had read that people did **when they** approached a king, or to remain standing.

" Well, my dear, what is your name? " continued the mayor.

" Katy Redburn, if you please, sir," replied **Katy,** with another courtesy.

" I am glad you have come to me with **this busi-** ness, Katy.   Mrs. Gordon speaks very handsomely of you."

" She is very kind, sir."

" You have lost your watch—have you, **Katy?** "

" My father's watch, if you please, sir;" and hav- ing gained a little confidence from the kind tones of the mayor, she proceeded to tell him the whole story of her adventure when she and Simon visited the pawnbroker's shop.

The mayor listened attentively to the **artless re-** cital, and promised to do all in his power to **regain** the watch.

" Were you alone, Katy, when you went to the pawnbroker's? "

"No, sir; there was one of your friends with me," replied she, with a simple smile.

"One of my friends?"

"Yes, sir; and he promised to see you about it."

"I am afraid you have been imposed upon, Katy."

"No, sir; he has often spoken to me about his friend the mayor."

"But who was he?"

"Master Simon Sneed."

"Sneed? Sneed?" mused the mayor.

"Yes, sir; Master Simon Sneed."

"Master? What is he? A schoolmaster?"

"Oh, no, sir. Everybody calls him master. He keeps store."

"Sneed? I never heard the name before. Where is his store?"

"In Washington Street. It says Sands & Co. on the sign."

"Oh, you mean the boy that makes the fires, sweeps out, and does errands. I remember him now," said the mayor, laughing heartily at poor Katy's account of Simon. "I never heard his name before; but he is the oldest boy of his age I. ever saw."

"He was very kind to me."

"No doubt he is a very good boy; but I supposed from your account of him that he was a member of the firm."

"Master Simon says the firm would not be able to get along without him," replied Katy, who began to have some doubts whether Simon was so great a man as he had represented himself to be.

"Master Simon is very kind to stay with them then, and I hope the Messrs. Sands will properly appreciate his merit. Now, Katy," continued the mayor, who had been writing while he questioned his visitor, "you may take this note to the City Hall, and deliver it to the city marshal: he will do all he can to recover your lost treasure."

"Thank you, sir," replied Katy, as she took the note.

"Now, good-by, Katy, and I hope you will always be as good as your candy is."

"I will try; good-by, sir!" and she left the library and passed downstairs.

John let her out very civilly, and seemed very grateful to her that she had not exposed his rudeness. She hastened to the City Hall, sure almost of recovering the watch, and gladdening her mother with the sight of it on her return home.

Simon Sneed, after parting with Katy, had felt a little uneasy in relation to the watch. He was jealous of his own credit, for he foresaw that Katy could not very well avoid telling the mayor that he had been with her at the time of the unfortunate transaction. Besides, he did not exactly like the idea of Katy's going to the mayor at all. Katy Redburn going to see the mayor! By and by everybody would know his Honor, and there would be no glory in being acquainted with him!

His conscience seemed to reprove him because he had done nothing toward the recovery of the watch.

What would his friend the mayor say if Katy should happen to tell him of his neglect?

"Here I am," said Master Simon to himself, as he entered the store, " a person of influence, enjoying the friendship of the chief magistrate of the city, and have not exerted my influence, or used my powerful friend, to redress the injury which this poor girl has received. I will correct my error at once, for if the mayor should happen to invite me to dinner some time, very likely he would reproach me for my neglect."

Having thus resolved to preserve his credit with the chief magistrate of the city, there was fortunately a lull in the waves of the Messrs. Sands & Co.'s affairs which enabled him to be absent for half an hour without serious injury to their business. He hastened to the pawnbroker's at which the robbery had been committed.

"I presume you know me, sir?" said Simon.

"I haven't that honor," replied the broker.

"Perhaps you may be able to recall the circumstance of a little girl presenting herself here with a silver watch."

"Well, I do."

"I was with her."

"Then I suppose you helped her steal it."

"Such an insinuation, sir, is unworthy a gentleman. I have come, sir, with a benevolent purpose, as I came before. In half an hour the history of that transaction will be conveyed to the mayor, who, allow me to inform you, is my friend."

"Your friend!" sneered the broker, who was not particularly impressed by the magnificent manners and the no less magnificent speech of Master Simon.

"The little girl has just gone with a note from Mrs. Gordon, of Temple Street, to seek redress of the mayor. I doubt not you will be prosecuted at once. You have an opportunity to save yourself."

"What do you mean by that, you young puppy?" said the broker angrily. "Do you mean to say I stole the watch?"

" By no means; only that you took what did not belong to you," replied Master Simon blandly.

" Get out of my shop! "

" Understand me, sir; I come as your friend."

" You are a fool, I believe."

" You have an undoubted right to your opinion, as I have to mine; but if you do not restore the watch within half an hour, you will be arrested for stealing—I beg your pardon, for taking what did not belong to you."

There was something in the earnest manner of Simon which arrested the attention of the broker, in spite of the former's high-flown speech. He was satisfied that something had been done, and he was disposed to avoid any unpleasant consequences.

" I spoke to a policeman about the watch," said the man. " I told him I had it, and if he found that such a watch had been stolen, it could be found at my shop."

" And if he did not find that such a watch had been stolen, you meant to keep it yourself," answered Master Simon, whose earnestness made him forget for a moment to use his high-flown words.

"Keep a civil tongue in your head," growled the broker. "I notified the police that I had it; that's enough."

"Perhaps it is; I will ask my friend the mayor about it;" and Simon moved toward the door.

"Stop a moment."

"Can't stop now."

"Here! I will go up to the city marshal with you. Maybe I made a mistake in keeping the watch; but if I did, it was only to prevent it from falling into the hands of some one less scrupulous than myself."

"Do I look like a thief?" asked Master Simon indignantly.

"It don't do to judge by appearances," replied the broker, locking his shop door, and walking toward the City Hall with Simon. "There are some very respectable looking thieves about."

Master Simon Sneed was satisfied with this explanation. He did not care to quarrel with anyone who acknowledged his respectability. In a few moments they reached the City Hall, and ascended the stone steps to the vestibule. As they did so, Katy entered from the opposite door.

"How glad I am to find you, Master Simon!" exclaimed she. "Can you tell me where the city marshal's office is?"

"Here it is, Katy," replied Simon, pointing to the door. "But what are you going to do?"

"I have got a note for the city marshal. The mayor gave it to me."

"You hear that, sir," said Master Simon to the broker, with becoming dignity. "This, Katy, is the man that has your silver watch; and he has consented to deliver it up to the rightful owner."

"Let me see the note," said the broker.

"No, I won't," replied Katy pretty sharply. "You are a naughty man, and I won't trust you with it."

"But I will give you the watch."

" Give it to me, and then I will show you the note," replied Katy, who was thinking more of getting the precious relic than of having the broker punished.

The broker took the watch from his pocket and handed it to her, and in return she produced the mayor's note.

" I suppose there is no need of your delivering this note now? " continued the broker, with a cunning smile.

" No; I don't care anything about it, now that I have got the watch," replied Katy, rejoiced beyond measure to recover the treasure.

" Well, then, I am somewhat acquainted with the marshal, and I will hand him the note, and explain the circumstances.   He will be perfectly satisfied."

Katy didn't care whether he was satisfied or not, so long as she had the watch.   But the broker entered the marshal's office, and they could not see him put the note in his pocket.

" I am so glad I got it! " exclaimed Katy.

" I doubt whether you could have recovered it if I had not used my influence in your favor," remarked Simon complacently. " I went to his office, and assured him my friend the mayor had already taken the matter in hand. I talked pretty severely to him, and he got frightened. After all, the best way is to use very pointed language to these fellows."

" I thank you very much, Master Simon; and I hope I shall be able to do something for you some time."

But Messrs. Sands & Co.'s affairs were suffering, perhaps, and Simon hastened back to the store, and Katy ran home to cheer her mother with the sight of the recovered relic.

CHAPTER X.

KATY, IN DISTRESS, FINDS A CHAMPION.

Now that she had recovered the precious watch Katy had nothing to engage her attention but the business of selling candy. The success that had attended her forenoon's exertions was gratifying beyond her expectations, and she felt as though she had already solved the problem; that she was not only willing but able to support her mother. She had originated a great idea, and she was proud of it.

Just as soon, therefore, as she had told her mother all about the recovery of the watch, she prepared another tray of candy, resolved to sell the whole of it before she returned. Her mother tried to induce her to stay in the house and rest herself, but her impatience to realize the fruits of her grand idea would not permit her to remain inactive a single hour.

" Now, mother, I shall sell all this candy before dark; so don't be uneasy about me. I am going to make lots of money, and you shall have everything you want in a few weeks," said Katy, as she put on her bonnet.

" I wish you would stay at home, and rest yourself; you have done enough for one day."

" I am not tired a bit, mother; I feel just as if I could walk a hundred miles."

" That's because you have got a new notion in your head. I am afraid you will be sick, and then what should we do? "

" Oh, I shan't get sick; I promise you I won't," replied Katy, as she left the room.

Unfortunately for the little candy merchant it was Wednesday afternoon, and as the schools did not keep, there were a great many boys in the street, and many of them were very rude, naughty boys. When she passed up the court some of them called out to her, and asked her where she was going with all that candy. She took no notice of them, for they spoke very rudely, and were no friends of hers. Among them was Johnny Grippen, whose acquaintance the reader made on the pier of South Boston bridge. This young ruffian led half a dozen others down the court in pursuit of her, for possibly they were not satisfied with the cavalier manner in which Katy had treated them.

"Where you going with all that candy?" repeated the juvenile bully, when he overtook her in Essex Street.

"I am going to sell it," replied Katy, finding she could not escape them.

"Give us a junk, will you?" said Johnny.

"I can't give it away; I am going to sell it, to get money for my mother."

"Won't you give a feller a piece?"

"I can't now; perhaps I'll give you some another time."

Katy's heart beat violently, for she was very

much alarmed, knowing that Johnny had not followed her for nothing.   As she made her firm but conciliatory reply, she moved on, hoping they would not attempt to annoy her. It was a vain hope, for Johnny kept close to her side, his eyes fixed wistfully on the tempting array of sweets she carried.

"Come, don't be stingy, Katy," continued Johnny.

"I don't mean to be; but I don't think I owe you anything," replied Katy, gathering courage in her desperate situation.

"What do you mean by that?" demanded the little ruffian, as he placed himself in front of her, and thus prevented her further progress.

"Don't stop me; I'm in a hurry," said Katy.

"Gi' me some candy, then."

"No, I won't!" answered Katy, losing her patience.

"Won't you?"

Johnny made a dive at the tray, with the intention of securing a portion of the candy, but Katy adroitly dodged the movement, and turning up a narrow alley way, ran off. Johnny was not to be balked, and followed her; and then she found she had made a bad mistake in getting off the street, where there were no passers-by to interfere in **her** favor.

"Johnny!" shouted one of the bully's companions; "Johnny, Tom Howard is coming."

"Let him come!" replied Johnny doggedly.

He did not half like the insinuation conveyed in the words of his associates; for to tell him, under the circumstances, that Tommy was coming was as much as to say he was afraid of him. Now, as we have said before, Johnny Grippen was a "fighting character," and had a reputation to maintain. He gloried in the name of being able to whip any boy of his size in the neighborhood. He was always ready to fight, and had, perhaps, given some hard knocks in his time; but he sustained his character rather by his talent for bullying than by any conquests he had won. On the whole, he was a miserable, contemptible little bruiser, whom no decent boy could love or respect. He talked so big about "black eyes," "bloody noses," and "smashed heads," that few boys cared to dispute his title to the honors he had assumed. Probably some who felt able to contest the palm with him did not care to dirty their fingers upon the bullying cub.

Sensible people, whether men or boys, invariably despise the " fighting character," be he young or old. Nine times out of ten he is both a knave and a fool, a coward and a bully.

On the other hand, Tommy Howard was one of those hearty, whole-souled boys who are the real lions of the playground. He was not a " fighting character," and being a sensible boy, he had a hearty contempt for Johnny Grippen. He was not afraid of him, and though he never went an inch out of his way to avoid a fight with him, it so happened they had never fought. He was entirely indifferent to his threats, and had no great opinion of his **courage.** Johnny had "stumped" him to fight, **and** even taken off his coat and dared him to come; but Tommy would laugh at him, tell him to put **on** his coat or he would catch cold, and, contrary to the general opinion among boys, no one ever thought the less of him for the true courage he exhibited on these occasions.

Johnny did not like to be told that Tommy was coming, for it reminded him that, as the king bully of the neighborhood, one of his subjects was unconquered and rebellious. But Johnny had discretion—and bullies generally have it. He did not like that cool, independent way of the refractory vassal; it warned him to be cautious.

"What's the matter, Katy?" asked Tommy, as he came with quick pace up the court, without deigning to cast even a glance at the ruffian who menaced her.

"Stand by, fellers, and see fair play, and I'll lick him now," said Johnny, in a low tone, to his companions.

"He won't let me go," replied Katy, pointing to her assailant.

"Go ahead, Katy; don't mind him."

"Won't you give me some candy?" said Johnny, stepping up before her again.

"Go ahead, Katy," repeated Tommy, placing himself between her and the bully. "Don't mind him, Katy."

As she advanced Johnny pushed forward and made another dive at the tray, but Katy's champion caught him by the arm and pulled him away.

"You mind out!" growled the bully, doubling up his fists, and placing himself in the most approved attitude, in front of the unwhipped vassal.

"Go ahead, Katy; clear out as fast as you can," said Tommy, who, though his bosom swelled with indignation, still preserved his wonted coolness; and it was evident to the excited spectators that he did not intend to "mind out."

"Come on, if you want to fight!" shouted Johnny, brandishing his fists.

"I don't want to fight; but you are a mean, dirty blackguard, or you wouldn't have treated a girl like that," replied Tommy, standing as stiff as a stake before the bully.

"Say that again, and I'll black your eye for you."

"Once is enough, if you heard me; but I will tell your father about it."

"Will you? Just say that again."

Somehow, it often happens that bullies want a person to say a thing over twice, from which we infer that they must be very deaf or very stupid. Tommy would not repeat the offensive remark, and Johnny's supporters began to think he was not half so anxious to fight as he seemed, which was certainly true. I have no doubt, if they had been alone, he would have found a convenient excuse for retiring from the field, leaving it unsullied by a black eye or a bloody nose.

My young friends will excuse me for digressing so far as to say that, in more than a dozen years with boys, in school and out, I have never heard of such a thing as two boys getting up a fight and having it out alone. There must be a crowd of bruisers and " scalawags " around, to keep up the courage of the combatants. Therefore, those who look on are just as bad as those who fight, for without their presence the fight could not be carried through.

Tommy Howard had said all he had to say, and was therefore ready to depart. He turned to do so, and walked several steps down the alley, though he kept one eye over his shoulder to guard against accidents.

" Hit him, Johnny! " cried one of the vagabond troop that always followed in the train of this young bully.

" He daresn't fight," replied Johnny.

" Nor you, nuther," added another of the supporters.

This was too much for Johnny. It cut him to the quick, and he could not stand it. If he did not thresh Tommy now, his reputation would be entirely ruined.

"Darsen't I?" exclaimed he. "Come back here;" but as Tommy did not come, he ran up behind him, and aimed a blow at the side of his head.

Katy's intrepid defender, who had perhaps read in some Fourth of July oration that "eternal vigilance is the price of liberty," was not to be surprised, and facing about, he warded off the blow. Johnny's imperilled reputation rendered him desperate. He had gone too far to recede, and he went into action with all the energy and skill of a true bruiser. Tommy was now fully roused, and his blows, which were strictly in self-defense, fell rapidly and heavily on the head of his assailant. But I am not going to give my young readers the particulars of the fight; and I would not have let Tommy engage in such a scene, were it not to show up Johnny as he was, and finish the portrait of him which I had outlined; to show the difference between the noble, generous, brave, and true-hearted boy, and the little bully, whom all my young friends have seen and despised.

In something less than two minutes Johnny Grippen, after muttering "foul play," backed out with a bloody nose, as completly whipped, and as thoroughly "cowed down," as though he had been fighting with a royal Bengal tiger.   His supremacy was at an end, and there was danger that some other bold fellow might take it into his head to thresh the donkey after the lion's skin had been stripped from his shoulders.

"If you are satisfied now, I'll go about my business," said Tommy, as he gazed with mingled pity and contempt upon his crestfallen assailant.

"You don't fight fair," grumbled Johnny, who could not account for his defeat in any other way. "If you're a mind to fight fair, I'll try it again with you some time."

"I don't fight for the fun of it.   I only fight when some cowardly bully like you comes at me, and I can't help myself.   When you feel like whipping me again, you needn't stop to let me know it beforehand.   But I will tell you this much: if you ever put your hand on Katy Redburn, or meddle with her in any way, I promise to pound you as handsomely as I know how, fair or foul, the very next time I meet you, if it isn't for seven years. Just bear that in mind."

Johnny made no reply; he was not in a condition to make a reply, and the victor in the conquest departed, leaving the bully to explain his defeat as best he could to his admirers and supporters.

"He did not hurt you—did he?" asked Katy, as Tommy joined her at the foot of the alley, where she had been anxiously waiting the result of the encounter.

"Not a bit, Katy.   He talks very loud, but he is a coward.   I'm sorry I had to thresh him, though I think it will do him good."

"I was afraid he'd hurt you.   You were very kind to save me from him, Tommy.   I shall never forget you, as long as I live, and I hope I shall be able to do something in return for you one of these days."

"Oh, don't mind that, Katy. He is an ugly fellow, and I wouldn't stand by and see him insult a girl. But I must go now. I told Johnny if he ever meddled with you again I should give him some; if he does, just let me know."

"I hope he won't again," replied Katy, as Tommy moved toward home.

This was Katy's first day in mercantile life; it had been full of incidents, and she feared her path might be a thorny one. But her light heart soon triumphed over doubts and fears, and when she reached Washington Street she was as enthusiastic as ever, and as ready for a trade.

CHAPTER XI.

KATY MEETS WITH EXTRAORDINARY SUCCESS.

"Buy some candy?" said Katy to the first gentleman she met.

He did not even deign to glance at her; and five or six attempts to sell a stick of candy were failures; but when she remembered the success that had followed her disappointment in the morning, she did not lose her courage. Finding that people in the street would not buy, she entered a shop where the clerks seemed to be at leisure, though she did not do so without thinking of the rude manner in which she had been ejected from a store in the forenoon.

"Buy some candy?" said she to a good-natured young gentleman, who was leaning over his counter waiting for a customer.

"How do you sell it?"

"Cent a stick; it is very nice. I sold fourteen

sticks of it to the mayor this forenoon.   He said it was good."

" You don't say so? Did he give you a testimonial? "

" No; he gave me half a dollar."

The clerk laughed heartily at Katy's misapprehension of his word, and his eye twinkled with mischief.   It was plain that he was not a great admirer of molasses candy, and that he only wanted to amuse himself at Katy's expense.

" You know what they do with quack medicines —don't you? "

" Yes, I do; some folks are fools enough to take them," replied Katy smartly.

" That's a fact; but you don't understand me. Dr. Swindlehanger, round the corner, would give the mayor a hundred dollars to say his patent elixir is good.   Now, if you could only get the mayor's name on a paper setting forth the virtues of your candy, I dare say you could sell a thousand sticks in a day.   Why don't you ask him for such a paper? "

"I don't want any paper, except to wrap up **my** candy in.   But you don't want to buy any candy, I see;" and Katy moved toward some more clerks at the other end of the store.

"Yes, I do; stop a minute.   I want to buy **six** sticks for my grandchildren?"

"For what?"

"For my grandchildren."

"You are making fun of me," said Katy, who could see this, though the young man was so pleasant and so funny she could not be offended with him.   "I don't believe your mother would like it, if she should hear you tell such a monstrous story."

The young man bit his lip. Perhaps he had a kind mother who had taught him never to tell a lie, even in jest. He quickly recovered his humor, however, though it was evident that Katy's rebuke had not been without its effect.

"For how much will you sell me the six sticks?" continued the clerk.

"For six cents."

" But that is the retail price; when you sell goods at wholesale you ought not to ask so much for them."

" You shall have them for five cents then," replied Katy, struck with the force of the suggestion.

" I can't afford to give so much as that. I am a poor man. I have to go to the theater twice a week, and that costs me a dollar. Then a ride Sunday afternoon costs me three dollars. So you see I don't have much money to spend upon luxuries."

" I hope you don't go out to ride Sundays," said Katy.

" But I do."

" What does your mother say to it? "

The clerk bit his lip again. He did not like these allusions to his mother, who perhaps lived far away in the country, and had taught him to " remember the Sabbath day and keep it holy." Very likely his conscience smote him, as he thought of her and her blessed teachings in the far-off home of his childhood.

"I will give you two cents," said the clerk.

"I can't take that; it would hardly pay for the molasses, to say nothing of firewood and my time and labor."

"Call it three cents, then."

"No, sir; the wholesale price is five cents for six sticks."

"But I am poor."

"You wouldn't be poor if you saved up your money, and kept the Sabbath. Your mother——"

"There, there! that's enough. I will take a dozen sticks!" exclaimed the young man, impatiently interrupting her.

"A dozen?"

"Yes, a dozen; and there are twelve cents."

"But I only ask ten."

"No matter; give me the candy, and take the money," he replied, fearful, it may be, that she would again allude to his mother.

Katy counted out the sticks, wrapped them up in a paper, and put the money in her pocket. If she had stopped at the door to study the young man's face she might have detected a shadow of uneasiness and anxiety upon it. He was a very good-hearted, but rather dissolute, young man, and the allusions she had made to his mother burned like fire in his heart, for he had neglected her counsels, and wandered from the straight road in which she had taught him to walk. If Katy could have followed him home, and into the solitude of his chamber, she could have seen him open his desk, and write a long letter to his distant mother—a duty he had too long neglected. We may not follow the fortunes of this young man, but if we could, we might see how a few words, fitly spoken, even by the lips of innocent youth, will sometimes produce a powerful impression on the character; will sometimes change the whole current of a life, and reach forward to the last day of existence.

Katy, all unconscious of the great work she had done, congratulated herself on this success, and wished she might find a few more such customers.

Glancing into the shop windows as she passed along, to ascertain whether there was a good prospect for her, she soon found an inviting field. It was a crockeryware store that she entered this time, and there were several persons there who seemed not to be very busy.

"Buy some candy?" said she, presenting the tray to the first person she met.

"Go home and wash your face," was the ill-natured response.

Was it possible she had come out with a dirty face? No; she had washed herself the last thing she had done. It is true her clothes were shabby, there was many a patch and darn upon her dress, and its colors had faded out like the "last rose of summer," but then the dress was clean.

"Buy some candy?" said she to another, with a sudden resolution not to be disturbed by the rudeness of those she addressed.

He took a stick, and threw down a cent, without a word. One more did her a similar favor, and she left the store well satisfied with the visit. Pretty soon she came to a large pianoforte manufactory, where she knew that a great many men were employed. She went upstairs to the counting room, where she sold three sticks, and was about to enter the work room, when a sign, " No admittance except on business," confronted her. Should she go on? Did the sign refer to her? She had business there, but perhaps they would not be willing to admit that her business was very urgent, and she dreaded the indignity of being turned out again. Her mother had told her there was always a right way and a wrong way. It certainly was not right to enter in the face of a positive prohibition, and at last she decided to return to the office and ask permission to visit the workshop.

" Please may I go into the workshop? " said she, addressing the man who had purchased the candy.

" Go in? why not? " replied he, placing his pen behind his ear, and looking at her with a smile of curiosity.

" Why, it says on the door, ' No admittance except on business.' "

" So it does. Well, I declare, you have got an amount of conscience beyond your station. No one thinks of taking any notice of that sign. Peddlers and apple men go in without a question."

" I thought you wouldn't let people go in."

" We don't like to have visitors there, for they sometimes do injury, and generally take off the attention of the men from their work. But you have got so much conscience about the matter, that you shall not only go in, but I will go with you, and introduce you."

" Thank you, sir; I won't give you all that trouble. I can introduce myself."

But the bookkeeper led the way to the door, and they entered a large room in which a great many men were busily at work.

" Here is a very honest little girl," said her friend, " who has the very best molasses candy I ever ate. If any of you have a sweet tooth, or any children at home, I strongly advise you to patronize her."

The bookkeeper laughed, and the workmen laughed, as they began to feel in their pockets for loose change. It was evident that the friendly introduction was to be of great service to her. She passed along from one man to another, and almost everyone of them bought two or three sticks of candy, and before she had been to all of them her stock was entirely exhausted. Katy was astonished at her good fortune, and the men were all exceedingly good-natured. They seemed disposed to make a pleasant thing of her visit, and to give her a substantial benefit.

"Now, my little girl," said the bookkeeper, "when you wish to visit the workshop again, you may enter without further permission; and I am sure the men will all be very glad to see you."

"But I want some of that candy," said one of the workmen. "My little girl would jump to get a stick."

"Then she shall have some," replied Katy, "for I will go home and get some more;" and she left the building and hastened home for a further supply of the popular merchandise.

"Oh, mother! I have sold out all my candy, **and** I want a lot more!" exclaimed she, as she rushed into the room, full of excitement and enthusiasm.

"Be calm, child; you will throw yourself into a fever," replied Mrs. Redburn. "You must learn to take things more easily."

"Oh, dear! I have only twenty sticks left. I wish I had a hundred, for I am sure I could sell them."

"Perhaps it is fortunate you have no more."

"But I must make some more to-night for to-morrow."

"Don't drive round so, Katy. Be reasonable, and don't think too much of your success."

But Katy could not stop to argue the matter, though, as she walked along the street she thought of what her mother had said, and tried to calm the excitement that agitated her. It was hard work to keep from running every step of the way; but her mother's advice must be heeded, and to some extent she succeeded in controlling her violent impulses. As it was, she reached the pianoforte manufactory quite out of breath, and rushed into the workroom as though she had come on an errand of vital importance to its occupants.

It required but a few minutes to dispose of her small stock of candy. The workmen all hoped she would come again, and she departed highly elated at her success.

"There, mother, I have sold all the candy. What do you think of that?" said she, as she entered her mother's room, and threw off her bonnet and shawl.

"You have done very well; I had no idea that you could sell more than twenty or thirty sticks in a day."

"It's a great day's work, mother; and if I can sell half as much in a day, I shall be satisfied.

Don't you think that now I shall be able to support you?"

" At this rate you can do much more; but, Katy, I tremble for you."

" Why, mother?"

" You get so excited, and run so, I am afraid it will make you sick."

" Oh, no, it won't, mother.   I feel as strong as a horse.   I am not tired in the least."

" You don't feel so now, because you are so excited by your success."

" I shall get used to it in a little while."

" I hope so, if you mean to follow this business."

" If I mean to?   Why, mother, what else could I do to make so much money?   See here;" and she poured the money she had taken upon the bedquilt before her mother.   " One dollar and thirty-six cents, mother!   Only think of it!   But I won't jump so another day; I will take it easy."

" I wish you would."

" I will try very hard; but you can't think how

happy I feel! Dear me! I am wasting my time, when I have to make the candy for to-morrow."

" But, Katy, you must not do any more to-night. You will certainly be sick."

" I must make it, mother."

" Your hands are very sore now."

" They are better; and I don't feel tired a bit."

" I will tell you what you may do, if you must make the candy to-night. When you have got the molasses boiled, you may ask Mrs. Colvin, the washerwoman, to come in and pull it for you; for you are not strong enough to do it yourself."

" I should not like to ask her. She's a poor woman, and it would be just the same as begging to ask her to give me her work."

" You don't understand me, Katy. She goes out to work whenever she can get a chance. Her price is ten cents an hour. You can engage her for one or two hours, and pay her for her labor. This is the only way you can get along with this business."

"I will do that. It won't take more than an hour."

Mrs. Colvin was accordingly engaged, though at first she positively refused to be paid for her services; but when Katy told her she should want her for one or two hours every day, she consented to the arrangement. Early in the evening the candy was all made, and Katy's day's work was finished. Notwithstanding her repeated declaration that she was not tired, the bed "felt good" to her, and she slept all the more soundly for the hard work and the good deeds she had done.

CHAPTER XII.

KATY PAYS HER DEBTS, AND TOMMY GOES TO SEA.

KATY's second day's sales, though not so large as those of the first day, were entirely satisfactory. The profits, after paying for the " stock " and for the services of Mrs. Colvin, were nearly a dollar, and her heart beat with renewed hope at this continued success. Her grand idea hardly seemed like an experiment now, for she had proved that she could make good candy, and that people were willing to buy the article. She met with about the same treatment from those to whom she offered her wares: one spoke kindly, and purchased by wholesale, and another spoke gruffly, and would not buy even a single stick. Here she was driven out of doors, and there she was petted, and made large sales.

So far as Katy's person and manners were concerned, she was admirably adapted to the business
she had chosen. She was rather small in stature
for one of her age, but she was very well formed,
and her movements were agile and graceful. Her
face was not as pretty as it might have been, but
her expression was artless and winning. Her light
brown hair hung in curls upon her shoulders, and
contributed not a little to make up the deficiency in
what the painters and sculptors would call a finely
chiseled face.

If she had been dressed in silk, and lace, and em-
broidery, I doubt not people would have called her
pretty, though in my opinion it does not make
much difference whether she was pretty or not; for,
after all, the best way to judge of a person's beauty
is by the old standard, " Handsome is that handsome does." But I have said thus much about
Katy's face and form in order to explain the secret
of her great success as a candy merchant. Hundreds of persons would buy a stick of candy of a

little girl with a pretty face and a graceful form, who would not do so of one less attractive. Though she was well favored in this respect, I believe it was her gentle, polite manners, her sweet voice, made sweet by a loving heart, that contributed most to her success. But above all the accidents of a good form, graceful movements, brown ringlets, and a pleasing address, she prospered in trade because she was in earnest, and persevered in all her efforts. A person cannot succeed in business by being merely good-looking, though this may sometimes be of much assistance. It is patience, perseverance, energy, and above all, integrity and uprightness, that lead to the true success.

Encouraged by her prosperity, Katy continued to sell candy with about the same result as had cheered her heart on the first two days. Her profits, however, were not so great as on those two days, and did not average above seventy-five cents a day, or four dollars and a half a week. This was doing exceedingly well, and she had every reason to be grateful for her good fortune.

At the end of three weeks rent day came round again, and Dr. Flynch called for the money. To his utter astonishment it was ready for him, and he departed without a single ill-natured word, though this was, perhaps, because he had a wholesome regard for the opinion of Mrs. Gordon. Two weeks later Katy found that her savings were sufficient to enable her to pay the month's rent for which Mrs. Gordon had given a receipt, and also the dollar which Grace had loaned her. These debts had pressed heavily on her mind. She knew that they were regarded as free gifts, and her pride prompted her to remove what she considered a stain upon her character. Till they were paid, she felt like a beggar.

Taking her money one day, she paid a visit to Temple Street. Michael opened the door, and received her with a smile. Knowing she was in favor with his mistress, he conducted her to the sitting room, where the portraits hung. Those roguish eyes of the lady, who somewhat resembled her mother, were fixed on her again. She was sure that her mother did not look like that picture then, but she was equally sure that she had, some time or other, cast just such a glance at her. The expression of the lady found something like its counterpart in her memory. Now her mother was sick and sad; she seldom smiled. But some time she must have been a young girl, and then she must have looked like that portrait. She felt just like asking Mrs. Gordon if that was her portrait, but she did not dare to do such a thing. While she was attentively watching the roguish lady's face, her kind friend entered the room, followed by Grace.

"How do you do, Katy?" said the former, with a benevolent smile.

"Quite well, I thank you, ma'am. I hope you will excuse me for coming again," replied she.

"I am very glad you have come."

"I was thinking of you the other day, and wishing I might see you," added Grace; " for the mayor told us a very pretty story about you."

" He was very good to me; and I never shall forget him or you," answered Katy warmly.

" I suppose you have come to get another receipt; but I told Dr. Flynch not to disturb you," said Mrs. Gordon.

" Oh, no, ma'am—I didn't come for that.   You were too kind to me before, and I have come now to pay you for that month's rent."

" Indeed? "

" Yes, ma'am; we have been able to earn money enough, and I am very glad that I can pay it," replied Katy, taking the four dollars from her pocket. " Here it is."

" No, my child; you shall keep it.   I will not take it."

Katy's cheeks flushed, for she did not feel poor and proud then.   She felt rich; that is, she was proud of being able to pay all she owed, and she did not like to be thought capable of accepting a gift—

of being the recipient of charity. But she knew the hearts of her kind friends, and left unspoken the words of indignation that trembled on her tongue.

" Please to take the money, ma'am," said she, her cheeks still red with shame.

" No, my child; you are a good girl; I will not take your money."

" I shall feel very bad if you don't, and it will make my mother very unhappy."

" Nay, Katy, you must not be too proud."

" I am not too proud to ask or to accept a favor, but please, I pray, don't make me feel like a beggar."

" You are a very strange child," said Mrs. Gordon.

" Indeed you are," added Grace.

" I shall not feel right, if you don't take this money. You know I promised to pay you at the time you gave me the receipt."

" I did not suppose you would; that is, I did not

think you would be able to pay it. Your mother
has got well, then?"

"No, ma'am; she is better, but she does not sit
up any yet."

"Then how did you get this money?"

"I earned it."

"You!"

"Yes, ma'am; selling candy."

"Is it possible? The mayor told me you were a
little candy merchant, but I did not suppose you
carried on such an extensive trade."

"I make a great deal of money; almost five dollars a week; and now I am able, I hope you will let
me pay you."

"If you insist upon it, I shall, though I had
much rather you would keep the money."

"Thank you, ma'am. I shall feel much better
when it is paid."

Mrs. Gordon reluctantly received the four dollars. It was a very small sum to her, though a very
large one to Katy. She saw that the little candy

merchant's pride was of the right kind, and she was not disposed to give her any unnecessary mortification, though she resolved that neither Katy nor her mother should ever want a friend in their need.

"I owe you one dollar, also," continued Katy, advancing to the side of Grace.

"Well, I declare!" laughed Grace. "If that isn't a good one!"

"I promised to pay you; and you know I would not take the money as a gift," replied Katy.

"I am aware that you would not, and you are the promptest paymistress I ever knew."

"With the dollar you lent me I bought the molasses to make the first lot of candy I sold. Your dollar has done a great deal of good."

"I am glad it has; but I don't want to take it."

"Won't you let me feel like myself?"

"Certainly I will," laughed Grace.

"Then let me pay my debts, and not feel just like a beggar."

"You are the queerest child I ever saw!" exclaimed Grace, as she took the dollar. "I am going to keep this dollar for you, and perhaps some time you will not be so proud as you are now, though I hope you will always have all the money you want."

"I think I shall, if my trade continues to be good," replied Katy, who, now that all her debts had been paid, felt a heavy load removed from her heart.

"You must bring your candy up here. The mayor says it is very good. I have a sweet tooth, and I will buy lots of it," added Grace.

"I will bring you up some to-morrow," replied Katy, moving toward the door, and casting a last loving glance at the mischievous lady in the picture.

"The mayor told me to ask you to call and see him again," said Mrs. Gordon. "He is very much interested in you."

"He is very kind;" and she bade them good-by.

Katy felt highly honored by the notice the

mayor had taken of her. Like Master Simon Sneed, she felt almost like calling him her friend the mayor; but she resolved to call upon him on her way home. He received her very kindly, told her what a mistake she had made in giving the pawn-broker his note, who had never delivered it to the marshal, and promised to buy lots of candy when she came with her tray.

When she returned home she found a message there from Tommy Howard, requesting to see her that afternoon. She did not feel like spending any more time in idleness, when she had so much candy to sell, but Tommy's request was not to be neglected; and, taking her tray, she called at his house as she passed up the court.

Tommy had been talking for a year about going to sea, and had been for some time on the lookout for a chance as a cabin boy or a reefer. He had told her his plans, how he intended to be a good sailor, and work his way up to be captain of some fine ship. She suspected, therefore, that he had found a chance to go to sea, and wanted to tell her all about it.

She found him at home, waiting her expected visit; but a feeling of sadness came over her when she saw his manly face, and thought how badly she should feel if he should go off on the ocean, and, perhaps, be drowned in its vast depths. He had been her friend and protector. Johnny Grippen hardly dared to look at her since the flogging he had given him, and Katy thought if he went away she should have no one to defend her.

"I am going to-morrow, Katy," said he, after he had given her a seat by the window.

"To sea?" asked Katy gloomily.

"Yes; I have got a first-rate ship, and she sails to-morrow."

"I am so sorry you are going!"

"Oh, never mind it, Katy; I shall be back one of these days. I wanted to tell you if Johnny Grippen gives you any impudence, to let me know, and I'll lick him when I come back."

" I guess he won't."

" He may; if he does, you had better tell his father."

" But where are you going, Tommy? "

" To Liverpool."

Katy started. Her grandfather lived there. After a moment's thought she conceived a plan which made her heart bound with emotion. She could send word to her grandfather, by Tommy, that she and her mother were in Boston; and then he would send over after them, and they could live in his fine house, and she should be as happy as a queen. Then she and her mother might be passengers in Tommy's ship—and wouldn't they have great times on the passage! And as her grandfather was a merchant, and owned ships, she might be able to do something for Tommy.

Under the seal of secrecy she related to her young sailor friend all the particulars of her mother's history; and he wrote down the names she gave him. Tommy promised to hunt all over

Liverpool till he found her grandfather; and to insure him a good reception, Katy wrote a short letter to him, in which she stated the principal facts in the case.

"Now, good-by, Tommy," said she, wiping away a tear; "I shall think of you every day, and pray for you too.   I hope there won't be any storms to sink your ship."

"We shan't mind the storms.   Good-by, Katy."

She felt very badly all the rest of the day, and her sales were smaller than usual, for her energy was diminished in proportion to the sadness of her heart.

CHAPTER XIII.

KATY EMPLOYS AN ASSISTANT.

As winter approached Katy realized that the demand for molasses candy was on the increase, and she found it necessary to make a much larger quantity. Mrs. Colvin still rendered her assistance "for a consideration," and the supply was thus made to correspond with the demand.

Mrs. Redburn's health, which had begun to improve with the advent of their prosperity, now enabled her to sit up nearly the whole day, and to render much aid in the household affairs, and especially in the manufacturing of the candy. The good fortune that had attended Katy's efforts brought many additional comforts to their humble dwelling; indeed, they had everything that they needed, and everything that any poor person would have required. But the fond mother had never been able to reconcile herself to the business which Katy followed. She dreaded every day lest the temptations to which it constantly exposed her might lead her astray. She loved her daughter with all her heart, and she would rather have died in poverty and want than have had her corrupted. She had every reason to believe that Katy was the pure and innocent child she had always been; but she feared, as she grew older, that some harm might befall her. She would rather bury her than see her become a bad person, and she hoped soon to be able to resume her own labors, and let Katy abandon her dangerous business.

Mrs. Redburn often talked with her about the perils that lay in her path, but Katy spoke like one who was fortified by good resolutions and a strong will. She declared that she knew what dangers were in her way, and that she could resist all the temptations that beset her. Whatever views the mother had, there seemed to be no opportunity to carry them out, for by Katy's labors they were fed, clothed and housed. She was her mother's only support, and the candy trade, perilous as it was, could not be given up.

Katy did not desire to abandon the business she had built up, for she was proud of her achievement. She was resolved to be good and true, and to her it did not seem half so perilous as to others. She had even indulged some thoughts of enlarging her business. Why could she not have a shop, and sell candy on a counter as well as in the street? She mentioned this idea to her mother, who was sure the shop could not succeed, for she was aware that her daughter's winning manners were more than half her stock in trade, and that her large sales resulted from carrying the candy to hundreds of people who did not want it enough to go after it. Therefore Katy gave up the shop at once, but she did not abandon the idea of enlarging her business, though she did not exactly see how it could be done. One day an accident solved the problem for her, and at that time commenced a new era in the candy trade.

One pleasant morning in November, as she walked up the court, she met Ann Grippen, a sister of Johnny, who stopped to talk with her. The Grippen family consisted of eleven persons. The father was a day laborer, and as his wages were small and he had a great many mouths to feed, they were, of course, miserably poor. The older children showed no ability or disposition to help their parents, but spent most of their time in strolling about the streets. Johnny was a fair specimen of the boys, as Ann was of the girls. She might have been seen almost any day with a well-worn basket on her arm, exploring the streets and wharves in search of chips, for Johnny was too vicious to do the work which more properly belonged to him.

"You sell lots of candy now—don't you?" said Ann.

"Yes, a great deal," replied Katy, who was not

disposed to spend her time idly, and in the company of one whose reputation in the neighborhood was not very good.

"Stop a minute—won't you? I want to speak to you."

"I will; but be as quick as you can, for I am in a hurry."

"Don't you think I could sell candy?" continued Ann.

"I dare say you could. Why don't you try, if you want to?"

"But I haven't got no candy; and mother can't make it, as you can. If you are a mind to let me have some, I will sell it for you, and you may give me what you like."

The idea struck the little merchant very favorably. There were a great many girls just like Ann Grippen, who were wasting their time about the streets and learning to be wicked. Why couldn't she employ them to sell candy?

"I will try you," replied Katy.

" Well, I'm all ready to begin."

" Not yet," said the little candy merchant, **with** a smile.

" Yes, I am."

" Your face and hands are very dirty."

" What odds will that make?" asked Ann, rather indignantly.

" Do you suppose anybody would eat a stick of candy after you had touched it with those dirty fingers? Your customers would be afraid of being poisoned."

" I s'pose I can wash 'em," replied Ann, who seemed still to regard it as a very unnecessary operation.

" It would be a good plan; and while you are about it you must not forget your face."

" I aint a-going to touch the candy with my face," added Ann triumphantly.

" Very true; but if people saw you with such a dirty face, they would be afraid your candy was **not** very clean."

" Any way you like. I will wash my face and hands both, if that's all."

" But that isn't all. Your dress is very dirty and very ragged."

" I can't afford to dress like a lady," said Ann, who had some of her brother's disposition, and under any other circumstances would have resented Katy's plain home thrusts.

" You needn't dress like a lady; but the neater and cleaner you are, the more candy you will sell."

" I will fix up as much as I can."

" Very well; if you will come to my house to-morrow morning, I will let you have some candy."

" How much will you give me for selling it? " asked Ann.

" I can't tell now; I will think about it, and let you know when you come."

Katy went her way, turning over and over in her mind the scheme which Ann's application had sug-gested to her. She might employ a dozen girls, or even more than that, and pay them so much a dozen for selling the candy.   She might then stop going out to sell herself, and thus gratify her mother. She could even go to school, and still attend to her business.

When she returned home at noon she proposed the plan to her mother.   Mrs. Redburn was much pleased with it, though she suggested many difficulties in the way of its success.   The girls might not be honest; but if they were not, they could be discharged.   Many of them were vicious; they would steal or be saucy, so that people would not permit them to enter their stores and offices, and the business would thus be brought into disrepute. Katy determined to employ the best girls she could find, and to tell them all that they must behave like ladies.

The next morning Ann Grippen appeared with her face and hands tolerably clean, and wearing a dress which by a liberal construction could be called decent.   She brought a dirty, rusty old tray, which was the best she could obtain; yet in spite of all these disadvantages the little candy merchant looked upon it as a hopeful case.

"Now, Ann, you must be very civil to everybody you meet," said Katy, as she covered the rusty tray with a sheet of clean white paper.

"I hope I know how to behave myself," replied Ann, rather crustily.

"I dare say you do;" and she might have hinted that there was some difference between knowing how to do a thing and doing it.   "I was only going to tell you how to sell candy.   If you don't want me to tell you, I won't."

"I should like to have you tell me, but I guess I know how to behave."

"You must be very civil to everybody, even when they don't speak very pleasant to you."

"I don't know about that," replied Ann doubtfully, for it was contrary to the Grippen philosophy to be very civil to anyone, much less to those who were not civil to them.

"When anyone buys any candy of you, you must

always say, ' Thank you '; and then the next time you meet the person he will buy again."

" How much you going to give me for selling? " demanded Ann, abruptly cutting short the instructions.

" Mother thinks you ought to have four cents a dozen."

" Four cents? My mother says I ought to have half, and I aint going to sell your candy for no four cents a dozen."

" Very well; you needn't if you don't wish to do so;" and Katy removed the sheet of white paper she had placed over the dirty tray.

" You ought to give me half I get," added Ann, rather softened by Katy's firmness and decision.

" Four cents is enough. I often sell a hundred sticks in a day."

" Well, I don't care; I will try it once."

" If we find we can afford to pay any more than four cents, we will do so."

Katy covered the tray again, and arranged two

dozen sticks on it in an attractive manner. After giving Ann some further instructions in the art of selling candy, she permitted her to depart on her mission. She was not very confident in regard to her success, for Ann was too coarse and ill-mannered for a good saleswoman. She hoped for the best, however, and after preparing her own tray she went out to attend to business as usual. In the court she saw Master Simon Sneed, who was sitting on his father's doorstep. She noticed that he looked sad and down-hearted, and when he spoke to her the tones of his voice indicated the same depression of spirits.

" Have you seen the mayor lately, Katy," asked Simon, as she approached.

" Not very lately."

" I should like to see him," added he, raising his eyes to her.

" Why don't you call upon him? You know where he lives—don't you? "

" Yes, but——"

Master Simon paused, as though he did not like to explain the reason. Katy waited for him to proceed; but as he did not, she remarked that he looked very sad, and she hoped nothing had happened.

"Something has happened," replied he gloomily.

"Nothing bad, I hope."

"I have left my place at Sands & Co.'s."

"Left it? Why, how can they possibly get along without you?" exclaimed Katy.

"It is their own fault; and though I say it, who should not say it, they will never find another young man who will do as much for them as I have done."

"I shouldn't think, in that case, they would have let you go."

"Nor I; but some men never know when they are well used."

"How did it happen?"

"I asked them for an increase of salary, and told them I could stay no longer unless they did so. And what do you think they did?"

"I don't know; I should suppose they would have raised your salary."

"No, Katy," added Simon bitterly. "Mr. Sands told me I might go; he wouldn't have me at any rate. Wasn't that cool? Well, well; if they don't know their own interest, they must bear the consequences. If they fail, or lose all their trade, they can't blame me for it. Now I have nothing to do; and I was just thinking whether my friend the mayor couldn't help me into a situation."

"I dare say he can. Why don't you call and see him at once?"

"I don't like to do so. He sees so many persons that I really don't think he would recollect me. I must get something to do, though; for my father is sick, and winter is coming on."

"How much salary did you get, Master Simon?" asked Katy, who highly approved his determination not to be a burden upon his father.

"Two dollars and a half a week."

"Is that all?"

"Yes; they ought to have given me ten. Even that was better than nothing."

"I was thinking of something, Master Simon," said Katy, after a pause.

"What, Katy?"

"I make four or five dollars a week."

"Is it possible!"

"If you have a mind to sell candy, I will furnish you all you want, so that you can make at least three dollars a week."

The lip of Master Simon slowly curled, till his face bore an expression of sovereign contempt. He rose from his seat, and fixed his eyes sternly upon the little candy merchant, who began to think she had made a bad mistake, though all the time she had intended to do nothing more than a kind act.

"What have I done, Katy, that you should insult me? Do you think I have sunk so low as to peddle candy about the streets of Boston?" said he contemptuously.

" Do you think I have sunk very low, Master Simon ? " asked Katy, with a pleasant smile on her face.

" Your business is very low," he replied, more gently.

" Is that business low by which I honestly make money enough to support my sick mother and my-self ? "

" It would be low for me; my ideas run a little higher than that," answered Simon, rather disposed to apologize for his hard words; for Katy's smile had conquered him, as a smile oftener will conquer than a hard word.

" You know best; but if I can do anything for you, Master Simon, I shall be very glad to do so at any time."

" Thank you, Katy; you mean right, but never speak to me about selling candy again. I think you can help me."

" Then I will."

" I will see you again when I get my plan arranged.   In the meantime, if you happen to meet my friend the mayor, just speak a good word for me."

" I will;" and Katy left him.

CHAPTER XIV.

MASTER SIMON SNEED MAKES A MISTAKE.

CONTRARY to the expectations of Katy and her mother, Ann Grippen returned at noon with her tray empty, having sold the whole two dozen sticks.

"Well, Ann, how do you like the business?" asked Katy.

"First rate. Here is twenty-four cents," replied Ann; and it was evident, from her good-natured laugh, that she was much encouraged by her success.

"You may give me sixteen; the other eight belong to you."

"I think I can do something at it," added Ann, as she regarded with much satisfaction the first money she had ever earned in her life.

"You can, if you work it right; but you must be

very gentle and patient; you must keep yourself clean, and——"

" Well, I guess I know all about that," interrupted Ann, who did not like this style of remark.

" Katy," said her mother, who was sitting in her rocking chair, by the fire.

" What, mother? "

" Come here a moment."

Katy crossed the room to her mother, to hear what she wished to say.

" You must not talk to her in that style," said Mrs. Redburn, in a tone so low that Ann could not hear her.

" Why not, mother?   I was only telling her how to do."

" But you speak in that tone of superiority which no one likes to hear.   You are but a child, as she is, and she will not listen to such advice from you."

Katy wondered what her mother would have thought if she had heard what she said to Ann the day before.   Yet she was conscious that she had

" put on airs," and talked like a very old and a very wise person.

" I suppose you would like to go out again this afternoon," resumed Katy, joining her assistant again.

" I don't care if I do."

" Well, come this afternoon, and you shall have some more candy;" and Ann ran home to get her dinner.

" I think my plan will work well, mother," said Katy, when she had gone.

" It has so far, but you must not be too sure."

" I mean to go out after dinner and hunt up some more girls, for you see I shall have no candy to sell myself this afternoon, when I have given Ann two dozen sticks."

" I hope you will not attempt to lecture them as you did her."

" Why, mother, I know all about the business, and they don't know anything."

" I doubt not you are competent to advise them;

but the manner in which you address them is more offensive than the matter. Your knowledge of the business makes you treat them as inferiors. You must not begin to think too much of yourself, Katy."

" No danger of that, mother. "

" I am afraid there is. Persons in authority, who are gentle and kind, and do not act like superiors, are more promptly obeyed, and more loved and respected, than those who are puffed up by their office, and tyrannical in their manners."

" But I am not a person in authority, mother," laughed Katy.

" You will be, if you employ a dozen girls to sell candy for you."

After Katy had eaten her dinner, and fitted out Ann Grippen, she left the house in search of some more assistants. She was well known to all the boys and girls in the neighborhood; and when she stated her object to one and another of them, she was readily understood. To help her cause, it had begun to be known that Ann Grippen had been seen with a clean face, selling candy in the street. She had no difficulty, therefore, in procuring the services of half a dozen girls, who were delighted with the plan, especially when Katy informed them of Ann's success.

On her return home she found that Simon Sneed had called to see her, and she immediately hastened to his house. When she knocked, he came to the door and invited her into the parlor.

" Well, Katy, I have hit upon something," said he.

" I am glad you have."

" I went down town after I saw you, and hearing of a place in Tremont Row, I went to apply for it."

" Did you get it? "

" Not yet, but I hope to get it. They agreed to give me three dollars a week if everything proved satisfactory; but they wanted a recommendation from my last employers."

" Of course they will give you one."

"No, they would not; they were offended because I left them."

"Then you asked them?"

"Yes, I went after one this forenoon, and they would not give it to me. I did not much expect they would, and I so informed Messrs. Runn & Reed, the firm to which I have applied for an engagement. I told them exactly how the case stood; that I had demanded higher wages, and the Messrs. Sands were angry with me for doing so, and for that reason refused the testimonial. They saw through it all, and understood my position. When I spoke to them about my friend the mayor, they looked surprised, and said a recommendation from him would satisfy them. So you see just how I am situated."

"Why don't you go to him at once and ask him for the recommendation?" said Katy, wondering why he hesitated at so plain a case.

But Master Simon had some scruples about doing so. He was old enough to know that it was rather a delicate business to ask a man in a high official station for a testimonial on so slight an acquaintance. The mayor was interested in Katy, though she did not presume to call him her friend. She had twice called upon him, and she might again.

"I don't like to ask him, Katy. I feel some delicacy about doing so."

"I should just as lief ask him as not, if I were you. I am afraid you are too proud, Master Simon."

"I am proud, Katy; that's just it. I was born to be a gentleman, but I submit to my lot. I am willing to sell my talents and my labor for money. If I can once get in at Runn & Reed's, I am sure they will appreciate me, and consider it a lucky day on which they engaged me."

"If you want me to go to the mayor's house with you, I will," said Katy, who did not clearly comprehend Simon's wishes.

"Well, I think I will not go myself," replied Simon.

"Why not?"

"I do not like to place myself in a humiliating posture before great men.   If I were mayor of Boston, I should like to do him the favor which I ask for myself.   When I am——"

"You haven't asked him, Master Simon."

"In a word, Katy, I want you to ask him for me. You will do me a great favor."

"I will," replied Katy promptly.

"The mayor is a very fine man, kind-hearted, and willing to help everybody that deserves help; and if he were not my friend, I should feel no delicacy in asking him myself.   You can state the case, and inform him who I am, and what I am; that you know me to be honest and faithful.   You can tell him, too, that I am a gentlemanly person, of pleasing address."

"But I can't remember all that," interposed Katy.

"Tell him what you can recollect, then.   He is an easy, good-natured man, and will give you the testimonial at once."

" Suppose you write a paper, just such as you want, Master Simon.   Then he can copy it."

" Well, I will do that."

Simon seated himself at a table, and, after considerable effort, produced the following piece of elegant composition, which he read to Katy:

" To whom it may concern:

" This may certify that I have been for some time acquanited with my friend Mr. Simon Sneed, and I believe him to be an honest and faithful young man, of gentlemanly bearing, pleasing address, and polite manners, who will be an honor and an ornament to any establishment that may be so fortunate as to secure his valuable services; and I cheerfully recommend him to any person to whom he may apply for a situation.

" Mayor of Boston."

" I have left a blank space for his Honor's signature," continued Master Simon, when he had read the modest document. " What do you think of it, Katy? "

" It is very fine.   What a great scholar you must be!   I should think you'd write a book."

" Perhaps I may one of these days."

" I will go right up to the mayor's house now," said Katy, as she bade him good afternoon.

Before she went, she returned home and nicely enclosed six sticks of candy in white paper as a present for Freddie, the mayor's little son.   On her way up to Park Street she opened Simon's paper, and read it.   It sounded funny to her, with its big words and fine sentences; and then what a puffing Master Simon had given himself!   She even began to wonder if there was not something about her gentlemanly friend which was not all right.

She reached the mayor's house, and as it was his time to be at home, she was conducted to the library.

" Ah, Katy, I am glad to see you," said he, taking her hand.

"Thank you, sir. I have brought this candy for Master Freddie."

"You are very good, and I suppose you are so proud that I must not make any offer to pay you for it."

"If you please, don't, sir," replied Katy, unconsciously taking Master Simon's testimonial from her pocket. "I don't want you to pay me in money, but you may pay me in another way, if you please."

"May I? What have you in your hand?"

"A paper, sir. You remember Master Simon Sneed?"

"No, I don't."

"The young man at Sands & Co.'s."

"Oh, yes; the young gentleman that uses so many long words."

"He has left his place, and wants to get another."

"Has he left it? Why was that?"

"He asked for more wages. He has found an-

other place, which he can have if he can get a tes·
timonial."

" Let him ask Sands & Co."

" They won't give him one, because they are so
angry with him for leaving them."

" That indeed."

" Master Simon wants you to give him one," continued Katy, who in her confusion was jumping at
the conclusion of the matter rather too hastily,
and before she had produced a proper impression in
regard to her hero's transcendent character and
ability.

" Does he, indeed," laughed the mayor.   " He is
very modest."

" He said, as you were his friend, you would not
object to giving him one."

" What have you in your hand, Katy?   Has he
written one to save me the trouble?" laughed the
mayor.

" I asked him to do so.   You can copy it off, if
you please, sir."

The mayor took the testimonial and proceeded to read it. Katy had already concluded from his manner that the business was not all correct, and she wished herself out of the scrape. He finished the reading, and then burst into a violent fit of laughter.

" Your friend is very modest, Katy,—my friend, Mr. Simon Sneed."

" I hope I haven't done anything wrong, sir? " stammered Katy.

" No, Katy; you have been imposed upon by a silly young man.   You meant to do him a kindness —in your heart you had nothing but kindness—and I think the more of you for what you have done, and the less of Simon for what he has done.   Did he think I would recommend him, when I know nothing about him?   He is a conceited puppy, and, in my opinion, a worthless fellow.   One of these days he will be ' an honor and an ornament ' to the workhouse, if he continues to do business in this manner."

"Dear me!" exclaimed Katy, frightened at the remarks of the mayor.

"Now, Katy, we will go to the store of the Messrs. Sands & Co., and find out about this young man. I will meet you there at half past four. Good-by, Katy. Freddie thinks ever so much of you now, and in his behalf I thank you for the candy."

Katy did not know exactly what to make of her position; but at the time fixed she was at the store of Sands & Co., where the mayor soon joined her.

"Now, Katy, you shall hear what his employers say of Master Simon," said he, and she followed him into the store.

The mayor stated his business, and inquired concerning the character of Simon.

"He is honest, and did his work very well," replied Mr. Sands.

Katy was pleased to hear this, and the mayor confessed his surprise.

"But he was an intolerable nuisance about the

store," continued Mr. Sands.   " With only a small amount of modesty he would have done very well; as it was, he was the biggest man in our employ. Our customers were disgusted with him, and we had been thinking of getting rid of him for a long time.   When he asked for more wages, impudently declaring he would leave if we did not accede to his demand, we discharged him.   In a word, I wouldn't have him round the store at any price."

" As I supposed," replied the mayor, as he showed Mr. Sands the recommendation Simon had written.

" This sounds just like him."

Katy pitied poor Simon now that she understood him, and she went home determined to tell him all that had passed between the mayor and herself.

CHAPTER XV.

KATY GETS A LETTER FROM LIVERPOOL.

MASTER Simon Sneed sat at the window when Katy returned, and she had to tell him all about it. She pitied him, poor fellow, and she hoped the lesson would do him good. She did not like to tell him so many unpleasant things, for they would wound his pride.

"Well, Katy, what did my friend the mayor say?" asked Simon, as he joined her on the sidewalk.

"I am afraid you will not call him your friend after this," replied Katy.

"Why? He had not the effrontery to refuse my reasonable request?"

"The what? Please to use words that I can

understand," said she, for she was not a little disgusted with Simon's big words, now she knew how much mischief they had done him.

" Didn't he give you the paper? "

" He did not."

" I didn't think that of him. It was shabby."

" He said he did not know you. But I showed him your paper, in which you had written down what you thought of yourself."

" Well, what did he say to that? " asked Simon, eagerly.

" I thought he would split his fat sides laughing. He didn't seem to believe a word of it."

" He didn't? I am surprised at that."

" He said you were a conceited puppy."

" I always took the mayor for a sensible fellow; I see I have been mistaken."

" He didn't like it because you sent me to him upon such an errand. He said you had imposed upon me."

" Go on, Katy; I may expect anything after

what you have said," replied Simon, with all the coolness and indifference he could command.

" He said he believed you were a worthless fel-low. Then he told me to meet him at the store of the Messrs. Sands & Co., and he would inquire about you."

" Then you went to the store? "

" We did; and when the mayor asked Mr. Sands about you, he said you were honest, and did you work well, but——"

" Notice that remark particularly. I hope you called the mayor's attention to it," interrupted Mas-ter Simon. " What else did he say? "

" He said you were a nuisance——"

" Observe how far his prejudices carried him. That man believed, if I stayed in the store, that I should supplant him and his partner. You see how far he carried his spite."

" But he said all the good he could of you, Si-mon," said Katy. " He said you were honest, and did your work well."

" Can a nuisance be honest, and do work well! Hath not a Jew eyes? " queried Mr. Simon, with dramatic fervor.

" He didn't say anything about Jews."

" I was quoting Shakspeare, the immortal bard of Avon. Katy, Sands knew that I was securing the respect and esteem of all his customers; and he knew very well if I should step into a rival establishment I should take half his trade with me," continued the injured Sneed.

" He said his customers were disgusted with you. You talked so big, and thought so much of yourself, he would not have you in the store at any price. But I should think that Runn & Reed would be glad to have you if you can carry so much trade with you."

" They cannot know till I have had a chance to show them what I can do."

" I hope you will soon have such a chance."

" There is one thing about it; when I do, Sands & Co. will see the mistake they have made. I think the ladies that visit their store will miss a familiar face. They used to insist upon my waiting upon them, though it was not exactly in the line of my duty to sell goods. Often was I called away from the bundle department to attend them. No one seemed to suit them but me. Why, it was only the day before I left that an elegant, aristocratic lady from Beacon Street made me go clear home with her."

" Why, what for? "

" To carry her bundle; but that was all a pretense."

" Did she invite you to tea, Master Simon? " asked Katy, who could hardly help laughing in his face.

" No; but she kept me quarter of an hour at the door."

" What did she say? "

" She was trying to make it out that I had brought the wrong bundle, and so she opened it in the entry; but it was only to keep me there."

" You think she was smitten? " laughed Katy.

" I have an opinion," replied Simon sagely. " There are a good many fine ladies will miss my face."

Katy didn't think any fine lady could be very much charmed with that thin, hatchet face; and she realized now that Master Simon was a great heap of vanity. She never thought before that he could be so silly. She wanted to tell him that he was a great fool, for she feared he would never find it out himself; but he was older than she was, and she did not think it quite proper to do so.

" I must go now," said Katy. " If you don't find anything you like better, you can sell candy, you know."

" Katy! " exclaimed Simon sternly.

" I am poor and proud, Master Simon; I am too proud to be dependent, or do anything mean and wicked; but I am not too proud to sell candy."

" I am," replied Simon, with dignity.

" Then yours is a foolish pride," replied Katy,

with a smile to soften the hard words; and she walked away toward her own house.

She felt thankful that she had no such pride as Simon's; and she had reason to be thankful, for when any person is too proud to do the work which God has placed within his reach, he becomes a pitiable object, and honest men will regard him with contempt.

Katy had to work very hard that evening, in making candy for her assistants to sell, and it was nine o'clock before she was ready to go to bed.

The next morning all the girls who had engaged to come appeared with their trays, and were supplied with candy. Katy instructed them very modestly in the art of selling, taking upon herself no airs, and assuming no superiority. Ann Grippen came with them, and seemed to be very much pleased with her new occupation.

At noon they all returned, though only two of them had sold out their two dozen sticks. Katy gave them further instructions in regard to the best places to sell candy, and when they came home at night, all but one had disposed of their stock. The experiment, therefore, was regarded as a successful one. The next day several other girls, who had heard of Katy's plan, came to the house, and wanted to be engaged. The little merchant could not supply them, but promised, if they would come the next day, to furnish them with a stock. Even now, the quantity manufactured required the services of Mrs. Colvin for three hours, and this day she engaged her to come in to help immediately after dinner.

I need not detail the manner in which Katy's trade kept increasing. In a fortnight she had more than a dozen girls employed in selling candy. She was actually making a wholesale business of it, and no longer traveled about the streets herself. By the first of December Mrs. Redburn had so far recovered her health as to be able to take the charge of the manufacturing part of the business, and Katy was permitted to go to school, though she supplied the girls in the morning and at noon, and settled all their accounts.

One day she received a call from Michael, Mrs. Gordon's man, requesting her attendance in Temple Street. She obeyed the summons, but when she met Mrs. Gordon and Grace she was alarmed to see how coldly and reproachfully they both looked upon her.

"I have heard a very bad story about you, Katy," said Mrs. Gordon.

"About me?" gasped she.

"Yes; and I was very sorry to hear it."

"What was it, ma'am? I hope I haven't done anything to lose your good will."

"I am afraid you have."

"I don't believe she did it, mother," said Grace. "She is too good to do any such thing."

"What is it? Do tell me."

"I have been told that a little girl, who sells candy, has been playing tricks upon passers-by in the streets; that she tells lies and deceives them."

"I never did such a thing!" protested Katy, her cheeks covered with the blush of indignation.

Mrs. Gordon explained the deception, and spoke in very severe terms of it. The trick had been played off on a friend of hers, who had told of it the evening before.

"When was it, ma'am?" asked Katy.

"Yesterday forenoon."

"I was in school then. Besides, I haven't sold any candy in the street for more than three weeks."

"I knew it wasn't she!" exclaimed Grace triumphantly.

"I was very unwilling to believe it," added Mrs. Gordon; "but the description seemed to point you out as the little deceiver."

"I wouldn't do such a thing, ma'am. If you inquire, you will find that I have been in school every day this week."

"I believe you, Katy. But can you tell me who it was?"

"I don't know, but I will find out;" and before

she took her leave she told the ladies how she conducted her business, which amused them very much.

"Who played this trick?" said she to herself, when she got into the street. "If I can only find out, I will discharge her. She will bring the business into contempt."

Of course no one would own it, and the only way she could find out was by watching them. It must be stopped, for, besides being too honest to allow such deception, Katy saw that it would spoil the trade.

When she got home she found a letter which the penny-post had brought, directed to her in large school-boy hand.

"It is from Tommy," exclaimed she, eagerly seizing the letter and retiring to a corner to read it.

"You and Tommy are great friends," said her mother.

"Yes, mother; but don't you see it came all the way from Liverpool?"

Mrs. Redburn sighed deeply at the mention of her native city, and a thousand memories of the past flitted before her. Katy broke the seal, and as this letter contained some very important information, my young readers may look over her shoulder while she reads it. It was as follows:

" LIVERPOOL, Nov. 13, 1843.

" DEAR FRIEND: I take my pen in hand to let you know that I am well, and I hope these few lines will find you enjoying the same blessing. I arrived to Liverpool safe and sound, and when I get home, I will tell you all about it. Just as we got into the dock I kept thinking about what you told me. They won't let us have any fires on board ship in the docks, so we all board ashore. I asked the man where we stopped if he knew such a merchant as Matthew Guthrie. He did not know him, and never heard of him. Then I went round among the big merchants, and asked about your grand-father. I asked a good many before I found one who knew him, and he said your grandfather had been dead ten years. I asked him where the family was. He said Mr. Guthrie had only two daughters; that one of them had run away with her father's clerk, and the other was married and gone to America. He said her husband belonged to Baltimore. This was all he knew about it, and all I could find out. We shall sail home in about three weeks. I thought you would like to know; so I wrote this letter to send by the steamer. Drop in and see my mother, and tell her I am well, and had a tip-top voyage over. No more at present from

> "Your affectionate friend,
>
> "THOMAS HOWARD."

Katy read the letter twice over, and then gave it to her mother, after explaining that she had told Tommy her story, and requested him to inquire about her grandfather. Mrs. Redburn was too much affected by the news from her early home to find fault with Katy for what she had done.

Both of them felt very sad, for while Mrs. Redburn thought of her father, who had lain in his grave ten years without her knowledge, Katy could not but mourn over the hopes which Tommy's letter had blasted.

CHAPTER XVI.

ANN GRIPPEN PLAYS TRICKS UPON TRAVELERS.

THE next day was Wednesday, and as school kept but half a day, Katy resolved to spend the afternoon in finding out which of her employees was in the habit of practicing the deception which Mrs. Gordon had described to her.   She could think of no one upon whom she could fasten the guilt, unless it was Ann Grippen, who, she thought, would be more likely to play such a trick than any other. After she had delivered their candy, she put on her things and followed the girls down to State Street, where they separated.   Ann went up Court Street, and Katy decided that she needed watching, and so she followed her.

It was a very tedious afternoon to the little wholesale merchant, but the dignity of the trade depended upon her efforts in seeking the offender. Ann entered various shops, and seemed to be having very good luck with her stock. At last she appeared to grow tired of her labors, and turned into an alley. Katy wondered what she was going to do there, for it was certainly no place to sell candy. She waited some time for her to come out, and when she heard her steps she placed herself at the corner of the alley in such a position that Ann could not see her face.

Presently she heard Ann crying with all her might, and crying so very naturally that she could hardly persuade herself that it was not real. She glanced over her shoulder at her, and discovered that she had broken the nice sticks of candy into a great many little pieces, and it was for this purpose that he had gone into the alley. Katy was indignant when she saw so much valuable merchandise thus ruthlessly mutilated, and the sales of it spoiled. She was disposed to present herself to the artful girl and soundly lecture her for the deceit and wickedness, but she wanted to see how the game was played.

"Boo, hoo, hoo!" sobbed Ann Grippen, apparently suffering all the pangs of a broken heart, which could not possibly be repaired.

"What is the matter, little girl?" asked a benevolent lady, attracted by the seeming distress of Ann.

"Boo, hoo, hoo!" cried Ann, unable to speak on account of the torrents of woe that overwhelmed her.

"Don't cry, little girl, and tell me what the matter is," continued the kind lady.

"Boo, hoo, hoo! I fell down and broke all my candy," sobbed Ann.

"Poor child!" exclaimed the sympathizing lady.

"My father'll beat me because I didn't sell it," added Ann.

"He is a cruel man. Are you sure he will punish you."

" Yes, ma'am," groaned Ann.   " He'll whip me almost to death if I don't bring home half a dollar."

" You can tell him you fell down and broke the candy," suggested the lady.

" He won't believe me; he'll say I sold the candy and spent the money.   Oh, dear me."

" You can show him the pieces."

" Boo, hoo, hoo!   Then he'll say I broke it on purpose, because I was too lazy to sell it; and then he'll kill me—I know he will."

" I will go and see him, and tell him about the accident.   Where do you live? "

" Down North Square.   He aint to home now," replied Ann, who was not quite prepared for this method of treating the subject.

" Poor child!   I pity you," sighed the lady.

" Oh, dear me! " cried Ann, exerting herself to the utmost to deepen the impression she had made.

" How much do you want to make up the value of your candy? "

" Half a dollar."

"There it is, poor child! If it will save you from abuse you are welcome to it."

"Thank you, ma'am. It may save my life," replied Ann, as she took the half dollar and put it in her pocket.

"What an awful liar she is!" said Katy to herself, as the lady hurried on, probably much pleased with herself as she thought of the kind act she supposed she had done.

Katy was curious to know what her unworthy assistant would do next, and she followed her down Hanover Street, and saw her stop before the American House. She could not believe that Ann would have the hardihood to play off the same trick again so soon; and she was very much surprised and very indignant when she saw her begin to cry with all her might, just as she had done before. While the deceitful girl's eyes were covered with her apron, in the extremity of her grief, Katy contrived to get on the hotel steps behind her, so that she could see and hear all that passed.

"What is the matter with that girl?" asked a gentleman, who presently appeared at the door, addressing another who was standing just behind him.

"It is the broken candy dodge," replied the second gentleman. "That trick has been played off a dozen times within a week."

"What does it mean?" asked the first. "I don't understand it."

The second explained the trick, precisely as Katy had just witnessed it in Court Street.

"Now, don't say a word," he continued. "I have a counterfeit half dollar in my pocket, and you shall see how it is done."

With this announcement of his purpose, he accosted Ann, who told him about the same story she had told the lady, and he finally gave her the counterfeit half dollar, which Ann did not suspect was a bad one.

"How abominably wicked she is!" exclaimed Katy, as she followed her up the street. "But I will soon spoil all her fun, and cut off her profits. I will certainly teach her that honesty is the best policy."

It was easier for Katy to resolve what to do than it was to do it, for the wicked girl could easily get her stock through another person. As she walked up the street Ann lightened her load by eating the pieces of broken candy, upon which she seemed to feed with hearty relish. At a window in Court Street Ann stopped to look at some pictures, when she was joined by another of the candy sellers, and they walked together till they came to an unfrequented court, which they entered. Katy could hear enough of their conversation, as she followed them, to ascertain that they were talking about the tricks Ann had practiced. In the court they seated themselves on a door stone, and as they talked and laughed about the deceit they ate the pieces of candy.

"There," said Ann, "I have made a dollar and ten cents this afternoon. You don't catch me walking all over the city for twenty-four cents, when I don't get but eight of that."

"I aint so smart as you," modestly replied Julia Morgan, the other girl.

"You'll learn," said Ann, as she took out her money and exhibited the two half dollars.

"I don't think people would believe me, if I should try that game."

"Try some other. I think I shall, for I've about used up the broken candy game."

"What other?"

"I have one," replied Ann, prudently declining to divulge her secret; "and when I've tried it, I'll tell you all about it."

"Why don't you try it now?"

"I would if my candy wasn't broken."

"I will let you have mine."

"Then I will."

"Give me fourteen cents."

"I will when I've done with it."

"No, you don't," laughed Julia, who justly inferred that if Ann would cheat one person, she would another.

But Ann was so much interested in the experiment that she decided to give the fourteen cents, and took the candy. Katy wondered what the new game could be, and wanted to see her carry it out, though her conscience smote her for permitting the lady to be deceived, when she could have unmasked the deceit. She resolved not to let another person be deceived, and followed the two girls into State Street, as much for the purpose of exposing Ann's wickedness, as to learn the trick she intended to play.

"Now you go away," said Ann to her companion, as she placed herself on the steps of the Merchants' Bank.

It was nearly dark by this time, and as there were but a few persons in the street, Ann did not commence her part of the performance till she saw a well-dressed gentleman approach, whereupon she began to cry as she had done twice before that day.

"Boo, hoo, hoo! Oh, dear me! I shall be killed!" cried she, so lustily that the well-dressed gentleman could not decently avoid inquiring the cause of her bitter sorrow.

"I haven't sold out," sobbed Ann.

"What if you haven't? Why need you cry about it?" asked the stranger.

"My mother will kill me if I go home without half a dollar."

"She is a cruel woman, then."

"Boo, hoo, hoo! She'll beat me to death! Oh, dear me! I only got ten cents."

"Why don't you fly round and sell your candy?" said the gentleman.

"I can't now; the folks have all gone, and it's almost dark. Oh, I wish I was dead!"

"Well, well, don't cry any more; I'll give you half a dollar, and that will make it all right;" and he put his hand in his pocket for the money for Ann.

"Don't give it to her," said Katy, stepping out

of the lane by the side of the bank. "She has deceived you, sir."

"Deceived me, has she?" added the stranger, as he glanced at Katy.

"Yes, sir. She has got more than a dollar in her pocket now."

"Don't you believe her," sobbed Ann, still prudently keeping up the appearance of grief.

"How do you know she has deceived me?" asked the stranger, not a little piqued, as he thought how readily he had credited the girl's story.

"Because I saw her play a trick just like this twice before this afternoon. She has two half dollars in her pocket now, though one of them is counterfeit."

"What do you mean by that, Katy Redburn?" demanded Ann angrily, and now forgetting her woe and her tears.

"You speak very positively," said the gentleman to Katy; "and if what you say is true, something should be done about it."

"She is telling lies!" exclaimed Ann, much excited.

"We can soon determine, for here comes a policeman, and I will refer the matter to him."

At these words Ann edged off the steps of the bank and suddenly started off as fast as she could run, having, it seemed, a very wholesome aversion to policemen. But she made a bad mistake, for, not seeing in what direction the officer was approaching, she ran into the very jaws of the lion.

"Stop her!" shouted the gentleman.

The policeman laid a rude hand upon her shoulder, and marched her back to the bank. In a few words the gentleman stated what had happened, and requested the officer to search her, and thus decide whether Katy told the truth or not. He readily consented, and on turning out Ann's pocket, produced the two half dollars, one of which the gentleman decided was a counterfeit coin.

"How could you know this was a counterfeit?" he asked of Katy.

"I heard a gentleman at the door of the American House, who knew the game, tell another that it was a counterfeit;" and she proceeded to give all the particulars of the two tricks she had seen Ann play off.

"I shall have to take you to the lock-up, my little joker," said the policeman.

"Oh, dear me!" cried Ann, and this time she was in earnest.

"Please don't do that!" said Katy, who had not foreseen this consequence of the game.

"I must; it is downright swindling."

"Please don't; she has a father and mother, and I dare say they will feel very bad about it. I promise you she shall never do it again," pleaded Katy.

"I must do my duty. This candy trick has been played a good many times, and has become a nuisance. I must lock her up."

"Save me, Katy, save me!" begged Ann, terrified at the thought of being put in a prison or some dreadful place.

" Why do you wish to save her? " interposed the gentleman.

" Because her mother will feel so bad; and she will lay it all to me."

Katy told him all about herself and about Ann, and he was so much interested in her, that he joined in pleading for Ann's release. The officer was firm for a long time, but when the gentleman declared that he should not appear against her, he decided to let her go, to Katy's great delight, as well as to Ann's.

Humbled by the peril from which she had just escaped, Ann promised never to be guilty of playing another trick upon travelers; but Katy was firm in her purpose not to supply her with any more candy. She did not dare to resent Katy's interference, for the terrors of the lock-up were still in her mind, and she did not know but that Katy might have her arrested and punished for what she had done, if she attempted to retaliate upon her.

Katy was shocked at the wickedness of her com-

panion, and as they walked home together she
tried to make her see the enormity of her offense,
and give her some better views of her duty to her
fellow-beings. Ann heard her in silence and with
humility, and the little moralist hoped the event
would result in good to her.

CHAPTER XVII.

THE SUN SETS, AND THE NIGHT COMES ON.

HAVING recorded the steps by which Katy had carried forward her now flourishing trade, from the dawn of the idea up to the height of its prosperity, we may pass over a year with only a brief note of its principal incidents.

My young readers may have supposed that Katy and her mother had gathered a great deal of money in the candy trade. It was not so, for as the business increased, and Katy's labors as a saleswoman were withdrawn, the expenses increased, and the profits were proportionally less. And then, neither Mrs. Redburn nor her daughter had a faculty for saving up much money, so that, though they made considerable, their prosperity permitted new demands to be made upon the purse. They hired two more rooms; they replaced the clothing and furniture which had been sacrificed under the pressure of actual want; they lived better than they had lived before; and Mrs. Redburn had availed herself of the services of a distinguished physician, whose attendance had cost a large sum. It is true they lived very well, much better than people in their circumstances ought to have lived. Therefore, notwithstanding their prosperity, they had saved but a small sum from the proceeds of the year's business. They were not rich; they were simply in comfortable circumstances, which, considering their situation when Katy commenced business, was quite enough to render them very thankful to the Giver of all good for the rich blessings he had bestowed upon them.

These were not all temporal blessings; if they had been, their success would only have been partial and temporary, their prosperity only an outward seeming, which, in the truest and highest sense, can hardly be called prosperity; no more than if a man should gain a thousand dollars worth of land, and lose a thousand dollars worth of stocks or merchandise. Both Katy and her mother, while they were gathering the treasures of this world, were also " laying up treasures in heaven, where neither moth nor rust doth corrupt." Want had taught them its hard lesson, and they had come out of the fiery furnace of affliction the wiser and the better for the severe ordeal. The mother's foolish pride had been rebuked, the daughter's true pride had been encouragd. They had learned that faith and patience are real supports in the hour of trial. The perilous life in the streets which Katy had led for a time exposed her to a thousand temptations; and she and her mother thanked God that they had made her stronger and truer, as temptation resisted always makes the soul. That year of experience had given Katy a character; it expanded her views of life, and placed her in a situation where she was early called upon to decide between the right and the wrong; when she was required to select her path for life.   She had chosen the good way, as Ann Grippen had chosen the evil way.

I do not mean to say her character was formed, or that having chosen to be good, she could not afterward be evil.   But the great experiences of life which generally come in more mature years, had been forced upon her while still a child; and nobly and truly had she taken up and borne the burden imposed upon her.   As a child she had done the duties of the full-grown woman, and she had done them well, had been faithful to herself.

Providence kindly ordains that the child shall serve a long apprenticeship before it is called upon to think and act for itself.   Katy had anticipated the period of maturity, and with the untried soul of a child had been compelled to grapple with its duties and its temptations.   As her opportunities to be good and do good were increased, so was her liability to do wrong.   She had her faults, great, grave faults, but she was truly endeavoring to overcome them.

Tommy had returned from his voyage to Liverpool, and joyous was the meeting between Katy and her sailor friend. It took him all the evenings for a week to tell the story of his voyage, to which Mrs. Redburn and her daughter listened with much satisfaction. He remained at home two months, and then departed on a voyage to the East Indies.

Master Simon Sneed, after Katy's attempt to serve him, did not tell her many more large stories about himself, for she understood him now, and knew that he was not half so great a man as he pretended to be. In the spring he obtained a situation in a small retail store, where there was not a very wide field for the exercise of his splendid abilities. He had been idle all winter, and when he lamented his misfortunes to Katy, she always asked why he did not sell candy. Once she suggested that he should learn a trade, to which Master Simon always replied that he was born to be a gentleman, and would never voluntarily demean himself by pursuing a degrading occupation. He was above being a mechanic, and he would never soil his hands with dirty work. Katy began to think he was really a fool. She could scarcely think him " poor and proud;" he was only poor and foolish.

At the close of Katy's first year in trade, a great misfortune befell her in the loss of Mrs. Colvin, her able assistant in the manufacturing department of the business. A worthy man, who owned a little farm in the country, tempted her with an offer of marriage, and her conscience (I suppose) would not not let her refuse it. Katy, though she was a woman, so far as the duties and responsibilities of life were concerned, was still a child in her feelings and affections, and cried bitterly when they parted. The good woman was scarcely less affected, and made Katy and her mother promise an early visit to her farm.

Katy's sorrow at parting with her beloved friend was not the only, nor perhaps the most important, result of Mrs. Colvin's departure, for they were de-prived of the assistance of the chief candy-puller.

Katy tried to secure another woman for this labor, but could not find a person who would serve her in this capacity. After a vain search, Mrs. Redburn thought she was able to do the work herself, for her health seemed to be pretty well established. Perhaps, she reasoned, it was quite as well that Mrs. Colvin had gone, for if she could pull the candy herself, it would save from two to three dollars a week.

Katy would not consent that she should do it alone, but agreed to divide the labor between them. The quantity manufactured every day was so great that the toil of making it fell heavily upon them; but as Mrs. Redburn did not complain, Katy was too proud to do so, though her wrists and shoulders pained her every night after the work was done.

This toil weighed heavily on Katy's rather feeble constitution, but all her mother could say would not induce her to abandon the work. For a month they got along tolerably well, and perhaps no evil consequences would have followed this hard labor, if everything else had gone well with Katy.   The girls who sold the candy had for some time caused her considerable trouble and anxiety.   Very often they lost their money, or pretended to do so, and three or four of them had resorted to Ann Grippen's plan of playing " tricks upon travelers."   She had to discharge a great many, and to accept the services of those whom she did not know, and who, by various means, contrived to cheat her out of the money received from the sales of the candy. These things annoyed her very much, and she cast about her for a remedy.

One day three girls, each of whom had been supplied with half a dollar's worth of candy, did not appear to account for the proceeds.   Here was a loss of a dollar in one day.   Such things as these are the common trials of business, but Katy, who was so scrupulously honest and just herself, was severely tried by them.   It was not the loss of the money only, but the dishonesty of the girls that annoyed her.

" What shall be done, mother? " said she anxiously, when the loss was understood to be actual. " I can't find these girls.   I don't even know their names."

" Probably, if you did find them, you could not obtain any satisfaction."

" I went to see one girl's mother the other day, you know, and she drove me out of her house, and called me vile names."

" I was thinking of a plan," continued Mrs. Redburn, " though I don't know as it would work well."

" Anything would work better than this being constantly cheated; for it is really worse for the girls than it is for us.   I have often felt that those who cheat us are the real sufferers.   I would a good deal rather be cheated than cheat myself."

" You are right, Katy; and that is a Christian view of the subject.   I suppose we are in duty bound to keep these girls as honest as we can."

" What is your plan, mother? " asked Katy.

"We will sell them the candy, instead of employing them to sell it for us."

"But they won't pay us."

"Let them pay in advance. We will sell them the candy at eight cents a dozen. Any girl who wants two dozen sticks must bring sixteen cents."

"I don't believe we can find any customers."

"We can try it. For a time, probably, the sales will be less."

"Very well, mother, we will try it; for I think it would be better to keep them honest, even if we don't sell more than half so much."

When the girls appeared the next morning to receive their stock, it was announced to them that the business would thereafter be conducted on a different basis; that they must pay for their candy before they got it, and thus become independent merchants themselves. Most of them were unable to comply with the terms, and begged hard to be trusted one day more. Katy was firm, for she saw that they would be more likely to be dishonest that day, to revenge themselves for the working of the new system.

The girls were not all dishonest, or even a majority of them, but the plan must be applied to all. Most of them went home, therefore, and shortly returned with money enough to buy one or two dozen sticks. As Mrs. Redburn had predicted, the effect of the adoption of the new plan was unfavorable for a few days. The obstinate ones would not buy, hoping to make the wholesale dealer go back to the old plan. After a week or two, however, they began to come back, one by one, and the trade rather increased than diminished, for many of the young merchants, having the responsibility of selling out all the stock imposed upon them, used greater exertion than before, and strong efforts almost always produced some success.

Thus the business went on very prosperously, though Mrs. Redburn and Katy were obliged to work very hard—so hard that the former began to experience a return of her old complaint. The affectionate daughter was frightened when she first learned of it, and begged her not to work any more.

" What shall I do, Katy? " asked she, with a smile.

" Let me make the candy," replied Katy. " I am strong enough."

" No, Katy, you are not. I am afraid you are injuring yourself now."

" I am sure I am not. But I can't bear to think of your being sick again."

" We must look out for our health, Katy; that ought to be the first of our earthly considerations."

" We ought, indeed, mother; so, if you please, I shall not let you pull any more candy."

" Shall I save my own health at the expense of yours? "

" I shall get along very well. I feel very strong."

" You are not very strong; I have reproached myself a great many times for letting you do so much as you have. I have felt the pain for a fortnight, and though I greatly fear I shall have a return of my complaint, I cannot let you do all this work. We are neither of us fit to perform such hard labor and both of us must be relieved from it. I shall go out to-morrow, and make a business of finding a person to do this work for us."

Mrs. Redburn did try, but she tried in vain. It was odd, queer, strange work, as the women called it, and they didn't want to do anything of the kind. Katy proposed that they should employ a man, and when they finally found one, he was a stupid fellow, and they much preferred to do the work themselves, to seeing him daub the house all over with the candy, and leave it half done.

They presevered, however, in their efforts to find a person, and after trying half a dozen, who could not or would not do the work, they gave it up in despair. But not long were they permitted to struggle with the severe toil which their circumstances imposed upon them; for on the night before Christmas, when a large demand for candy was anticipated, and both of them had worked very hard, Mrs. Redburn fainted and fell upon the floor. It was in this manner that she had been taken at the commencement of her former long sickness, and to Katy the future looked dark and gloomy. But she did not give up. She applied herself, with all her energies, to the restoration of her mother; and when she was partially conscious, she attempted to conduct her to the bed. The poor woman's strength was all gone, and Katy was obliged to call in Mrs. Howard to assist her.

Mrs. Redburn suffered the most severe and racking pains through the night, and at about twelve o'clock Katy went to Mr. Sneed's house, and calling up Simon, begged him to go for a doctor. But the physician's art seemed powerless to soothe her. All night long the devoted daughter, like an angel of mercy, hovered around the bed, and did all she could in vain attempts to ease the sufferer's pain.

Poor Katy! The sun of prosperity had set, and the night of adversity was coming on.

CHAPTER XVIII.

KATY STRUGGLES BRAVELY THROUGH A SERIES OF TRIALS.

THE morning sun rose clear and bright, casting a flood of light into the chamber of the sick mother, watched over by the beloved child. It was Christmas, and all over the Christian world arose pæans of praise for the birth of the Saviour. The sufferer was conscious of the fact, and a sweet smile played upon her lips as she thought of Jesus, that he had lived and died for her. Pain, that could rack the bones and triumph over the weak body, was powerless to subdue the loving, trusting spirit that reposed gently on Him who has invited the weary to a present and an eternal rest.

" Katy," said Mrs. Redburn, in a faint whisper.

" I am here, mother," replied she, bending over

her, and endeavoring to anticipate her unspoken desire.

"Is the hymn book on the table?"

"Here it is, mother."

"Won't you read me a hymn?"

"What shall I read?" asked Katy, who could with difficulty keep back the flood of tears that rose up from her heart.

"'Come, said Jesus' sacred voice.'"

Katy opened the book to the beautiful hymn commencing with this line, and in a voice broken by the emotions she could not wholly control, she read it through. The smile that played on her mother's face showed how deep and pure was the consolation she derived from the touching poetry. She could smile while racking pains tortured her frame, while her frail body seemed hardly to retain its hold upon mortality. How blessed is the hope that pours its heavenly balm into the wounds of the sufferer!

Poor Katy was painfully impressed by the appearance and conduct of her mother. She had never before seen her so calm and resigned to those dreadful sufferings. She had heard her complain and murmur at her hard lot, and wonder why she should be thus sorely afflicted. She feared that some appalling event, which she dared not define and call by its name, was about to happen. She dared not think of the future, and she wondered that her mother could be so calm while she endured so much.

"Katy," said Mrs. Redburn, after the long silence that followed the reading of the hymn, "I feel very weak and ill. Take my hand."

"You are burning up with fever!" exclaimed Katy, as she clasped the hand, and felt the burning, throbbing brow of her mother.

"I am; but do not be alarmed, Katy. Can you be very calm?"

"I will try."

"For I feel very sick, but I am very happy. I can almost believe that the triumph of faith has already begun in my soul. The world looks very dim to me."

" Nay, mother, don't say so."

" I only mean that as heaven seems nearer, my hold upon earth is less strong. You must be very resolute, my child, for I feel as though the sands of life were fast ebbing out; and that in a few hours more I shall be ' where the wicked cease from troubling, and the weary are at rest.' If it were not for leaving you, Katy, I could wish to bid farewell to earth, and go up to my eternal home, even on this bright, beautiful Christmas day."

" Oh, mother! " sobbed Katy, unable any longer to restrain the expression of her emotion.

" Do not weep, my child; I may be mistaken; yet I feel as though God was about to end my sufferings on earth, and I am willing to go."

" Oh, no, mother! It cannot be! " exclaimed Katy, gazing earnestly, through her tearful eyes, upon the pale but flushed cheek of the patient sufferer.

" I only wish to prepare you for the worst. I may get well; and for your sake, I have prayed that I may. And, Katy, I have never before felt prepared to leave this world, full of trial and sorrow as it has been to me. Whatever of woe, and want, and disappointment it has been my lot to confront, has been a blessing in disguise. I feel like a new creature. I feel reconciled to live or die, as God ordains."

" Do not look on the dark side, mother," sobbed Katy.

" Nay, child, I am looking on the bright side," returned Mrs. Redburn faintly. " Everything looks bright to me now. Life looks bright, and I feel that I could be happy for many years with you, for you have been a good daughter. Death looks bright, for it is the portal of the temple eternal in the heavens, where is joy unspeakable. I am too weak to talk more, Katy; you may read me a chapter from the New Testament."

The devoted daughter obeyed this request, and

she had scarcely finished the chapter before the girls came for their candy. She was unwilling to leave her mother alone even for a minute; so she sent one of them over to request the attendance of Mrs. Howard, and the good woman took her place by the side of the sufferer.

Katy, scarcely conscious what she was doing,—for her heart was with her mother,—supplied each girl with her stock of candy, and received the money for it.

"You need not come to-morrow," she said to them, as they were departing.

"Not come!" exclaimed several. "What shall we do for candy?"

"We cannot make any now; my mother is very sick."

"I get my living by selling candy," said one of them. "I shan't have anything to pay my board if I can't sell candy."

"Poor Mary! I am sorry for you."

This girl was an orphan whose mother had

recently died, and she had taken up the business of selling candy, which enabled her to pay fifty cents a week for her board, at the house of a poor widow. Katy knew her history, and felt very sad as she thought of her being deprived of the means of support.

"I don't know what I shall do," sighed Mary.

"I have to take care of my mother now, and shall not have time to make candy," said Katy.

"Do you mean to give up for good?" asked one of them.

"I don't know."

This question suggested some painful reflections to Katy. If they stopped making candy, she and her mother, as well as orphan Mary, would be deprived of the means of support. She trembled as she thought of the future, even when she looked forward only a few weeks. There was not more than ten dollars in the house, for they had but a short time before paid for their winter's coal, and at considerable expense largely replenished their wardrobes.   The rent would be due in a week, and it would require more than half they had to pay it.

Katy was appalled as she thought of the low state of their purse, and dreaded lest some fearful calamity might again overtake them.   It was plain to her that she could not give up her business, even for a week, without the danger of being again reduced to actual want.   She therefore reversed her decision, and told the girls they might come as usual the next day.

When they had gone she shed a few bitter tears at the necessity which the circumstances imposed upon her of working while her heart revolted at the idea of being anywhere but at the bedside of her sick mother.   Then she lamented that they had not dispensed with many articles of luxury while they had plenty of money, and saved more of it for such a sad time as the present.   But it was of no use to repine; she had only to make the best of her situation.

Amid all these discouragements came a bright

ray of sunshine—the brightest that could possibly have shone on the pathway of the weeping daughter.

Early in the forenoon came the physician, who carefully examined his patient, speaking cheerfully and kindly to her all the while. The sufferer watched his expression very narrowly, as he bent over her and questioned her in regard to her pains. He looked very serious, which Mrs. Redburn interpreted as unfavorable to her recovery, not considering that he was engaged in profound thought, and therefore his countenance would naturally wear an earnest look. Presently she sent Katy to get her some drink, not because she wanted it, but to procure her absence for a short time.

"Do you think I shall get well?" asked Mrs. Redburn anxiously, as soon as the door closed behind Katy.

"A person who is very sick is, of course, always in danger, which may be more or less imminent," replied the doctor, with professional indirectness.

"I beg of you, doctor, do not conceal from me my true situation."

"I cannot foresee the result, my good woman."

"Do you think there is any hope for me?"

"Certainly there is."

"Tell me, I implore you, what you think of my case," pleaded the sufferer, in feeble tones. "I felt this morning that my end was very near."

"Oh, no; it is not so bad as that. I should say you had as many as five chances in ten to be on your feet in a fortnight."

"Do you think so?"

"I do not regard your case as a critical one."

"I wish you had told me so last night. It would have saved my poor child a very bitter pang."

"I was not aware that you thought yourself alarmingly sick, or I certainly should; for such an opinion on your part would do more to bring about a fatal result than could be counteracted by the most skillful treatment. A physician does not hold

the issues of life and death; he can only assist
nature, as the patient may by a cheerful view of his
case. This is not your old complaint; you have
taken cold, and have considerable fever; but I think
it is a very hopeful case."

The return of Katy interrupted the conversation; but the doctor's opinion was immediately im-
parted to her, and it sent a thrill of joy to her heart.

"I was low-spirited this morning, Katy," said
Mrs. Redburn, when the physician had gone. "I
really felt as though my end was rapidly approaching. I am sorry I mentioned my thoughts to you."

"It was all for the best, I suppose," replied
Katy.

But Mrs. Redburn was very sick; and even now
the disease might have a fatal termination. The
best of care would be required to restore her to
health, and Katy was very anxious. Her mother
was still suffering the most acute pain.

The doctor had left a prescription, and Katy was
again obliged to call in Mrs. Howard while she went

to the apothecary's to procure it; but the good woman declared she was glad to come, and would bring her work and stay all the forenoon. The medicine, when obtained, to some extent relieved the sufferer's pain.

As her presence was not required in the chamber, Katy went downstairs to what she called the candy room. She had an hour or two to spare, and she put on the kettle with the intention of making a part of the next day's candy. She was nearly worn out by watching and anxiety, and not fit to perform such hard work; but weak and weary as she felt, her spirit was still earnest, and she resolutely commenced her labors.

At noon she had made half the quantity required. Mrs. Howard was then obliged to go home, and attend to her own family, for she had two children besides Tommy, who had not yet returned from the East Indies. Mrs. Redburn was very restless during the afternoon, and could not be left alone for more than a short time at once. Mrs.

Howard had promised to come in in the evening and make the rest of the candy; but Charley came home from school quite sick, seemingly threatened with the scarlet fever, so that she could not keep her promise. Mrs. Sneed, however, dropped in, and consented to remain for two hours, which enabled Katy to make the next day's supply of the candy.

By this time the poor girl was completely worn out. Her resolute will, even, could no longer impart its strength to the body. Her mother worried sadly about her, and finally induced her to lie down on the bed by her side, on condition that she should be awakened in an hour. In this manner she obtained a few hours sleep during the night; but these severe labors were a fearful task to be imposed upon a mere child.

The next day Mrs. Redburn, who could not fail to observe Katy's pale face and sunken eye, fretted so much about her that she was obliged to promise she would not attempt to make any more candy.

Mrs. Howard's son was still very sick, so that she was unable to render much assistance. The rest of the neighbors, though kindly disposed, had their own families to care for, and could do very little for others.

With what slight aid her friends could afford, Katy struggled through a week, when Dr. Flynch appeared, and demanded the rent. There was but little more than money enough left to pay it, but Katy would not ask him for any indulgence, and paid him in full.

In a few days more the purse was empty. Katy's most dreaded hour had come. She had no money, and almost every day some new thing was required for her mother. But now she had friends, and she determined to use them, as all true friends wish to be used in the day of sorrow and trial. After considerable debate with herself, she decided to apply to Mrs. Gordon for a loan of twenty dollars. She was still poor and proud, and she could not endure the thought of asking a loan, which might be regarded as a gift, or which, by her own inability to pay it, might virtually become such; therefore she proposed to present her father's silver watch as security for the payment of the debt.

CHAPTER XIX.

KATY RESORTS TO A LOAN.

KATY was not at all pleased with the mission which her duty seemed to impose upon her. Again she felt the crushing weight of poverty, and pride rose up to throw obstacles in her path. She was a child of twelve, and to ask a loan of twenty dollars, though she offered sufficient security for the payment of the debt, seemed like demanding a great deal of her friends—like inviting them to repose a vast amount of confidence in her ability and honesty. They would not want the watch; it would be of no value to them; and the more she considered the matter, the more like an act of charity appeared the favor she was about to ask.

More than once on her way to Temple Street did she stop short, resolved to get the money of some other person—the grocer, Mr. Sneed, or even of a pawnbroker; but as often she rebuked the pride that tormented her like a demon, and went forward again. She stood some time at Mrs. Gordon's door before she had the resolution to ring the bell.

"What right have I to be so proud?" said she, grasping the bell handle. "I must get this money, or my mother may suffer."

She rang with a force that must have astonished Michael, and led him to think some extraordinary character had arrived; for he ran to the door at full speed, and burst out into a violent fit of laughter, when he saw no one but the little candy merchant.

"Good-morning to you, Katy. Are you nervous this morning?" said he.

"Good-morning, Michael. I am not very nervous."

"I thought you would pull down the bell," he added good-naturedly.

"I didn't mean to, Michael; I hope you will excuse me if I did any harm."

"Not a bit of harm; but you're looking as sober as a deacon. What ails you, Katy?"

"I feel very sad, Michael; for my mother is very sick, and I don't know as she will ever get well."

"Indeed? I'm sorry to hear that of her;" and Michael, whatever he felt, looked very much concerned about Mrs. Redburn's health.

"Is Mrs. Gordon at home?"

"She isn't."

"Is Miss Grace?"

"Neither of them; they went to Baltimore ten days ago; but I am expecting them back every day."

Katy's heart sunk within her; for now that Mrs. Gordon was not at hand, she did not feel like asking any other person; and if the case had not been urgent, she would have been satisfied to return home, and regard the lady's absence as a sufficient excuse for not procuring the money.

"You want to see her very much?" asked Michael.

" Very much, indeed."

" Can I be of any service to you? "

" No, Michael."

" Perhaps I can, Katy."

" No, I'm much obliged to you."

" If it's anything in the house you want, I can get it for you."

" No, I must see Mrs. Gordon."

" If it's any nice preserves or jelly you want just say the word, and I'll bring it to you at once."

" I do not want anything of that kind. Do you think Mrs. Gordon will return by to-morrow? "

" I thought she would be here yesterday, and she may come to-night."

" Very well; I will, perhaps, call again to-morrow;" and she turned to leave.

" I'll tell Mrs. Gordon you came. Stop a minute, Katy. Won't you tell me what you want? "

" I would rather not, Michael; but I will come again to-morrow."

" See here, Katy; maybe you're short of money. If you are, I have a matter of three hundred dollars in the Savings Bank; and you may be sure you shall have every cent of it if you want it."

This was a very liberal offer, though it is probable he did not think she would want any considerable portion of it, or that she could even comprehend the meaning of so large a sum. Katy was sorely tempted to negotiate with him for the loan; but she was not sure that it would be proper to borrow money of the servant, and perhaps Mrs. Gordon would not like it.

" I thank you, Michael; you are very kind, but I think I would rather see Mrs. Gordon."

" I have a matter of five or six dollars in my pocket now, and if that 'll be of any service to you, take it and welcome."

Katy stopped to think. A few dollars would be all that she needed before the return of Mrs. Gordon; and yet she did not feel like accepting it. What would the lady say on her return, when told that she had borrowed money of her servant? Yet the servant had a kind heart, and really desired to serve her. Was it not pride that prevented her from accepting his offer? Did she not feel too proud to place herself under obligations to the servant? She felt rebuked at her presumption; for what right had she to make such distinctions? If she had been a lady, like Mrs. Gordon, she might have been excusable for cherishing such a pride; but instead she was a poor girl; she was actually in want.

"Michael, you are so good, that I will tell you my story," said she, conquering her repugnance.

"Just come in the house, then;" and he led her into the sitting room, being, in the absence of the mistress, the lord and master of the mansion, and feeling quite at home in that position.

In a few words she explained to him her situation, though her rebellious pride caused her to paint the picture in somewhat brighter colors than the truth would fully justify. She stated her intention to borrow twenty dollars of Mrs. Gordon, and offer her the watch as security, at the same time exhibiting the cherished treasure.

" Now, Michael, if you will lend me three dollars till Mrs. Gordon returns, I will pay you then, for I know she will let me have the money; or at least let me have enough to pay you," continued she when she had finished her narrative.

" Indeed I will, Katy! " exclaimed he, promptly pulling out his wallet.   " And if you will come at this time to-morrow, you shall have the whole 'wenty dollars."

" Thank you, Michael."

" There's six dollars; take it, Katy, and my blessing with it."

" Only three dollars, Michael," replied Katy, firmly.

Michael insisted, but all his persuasion would not induce her to accept more than the sum she had mentioned, and he was reluctantly compelled to yield the point.

"Here is the watch, Michael; you shall keep that till I pay you."

"Is it me!" exclaimed he, springing to his feet, with an expression very like indignation on his countenance. "Sure, you don't think I'd take the watch!"

"Why not you as well as Miss Gordon?" asked Katy.

"She didn't take it," replied Michael triumphantly. "You couldn't make her take it, if you try a month. Don't I know Mrs. Gordon?"

"But please to take it; I should feel much better if you would."

"Bad luck to me if I do. I wouldn't take it to save my neck from the gallows. Where's my Irish heart? Did I leave it at home, or did I bring it with me to America?"

"If you will not take it, Michael——"

"I won't!"

"If you won't, I will say no more about it," replied Katy, as she returned the watch to her pocket.

" You have got a very kind heart, and I shall never forget you as long as I live."

Katy, after glancing at the portrait of the roguish lady that hung in the room, took leave of Michael, and hastened home. On her way, she could not banish the generous servant from her mind. She could not understand why he should be so much interested in her as to offer the use of all he had, and she was obliged to attribute it all to the impulses of a kind heart. If she had been a little older she might have concluded that the old maxim, slightly altered, would explain the reason: " Like mistress, like man;" that the atmosphere of kindness and charity that pervaded the house had inspired even the servants.

"Where have you been, Katy?" asked Mrs. Redburn, as she entered the sick chamber, and Mrs. Sneed hastened home.

"I have been to Mrs. Gordon."

" What for? "

Katy did not like to tell. She knew it would

make her mother feel very unhappy to know that she had borrowed money of Mrs. Gordon's servant.

" Oh, I went up to see her," replied Katy.

" No matter, if you don't like to tell me," faintly replied Mrs. Redburn.

" I will tell you, mother," answered Katy, stung by the gentle rebuke contained in her mother's words.

" I suppose our money is all gone," sighed the sick woman.

" No, mother; see here! I have three dollars," and Katy pulled out her portemonnaie, anxious to save her even a moment of uneasiness.

But in taking out the money she exhibited the watch also, which at once excited Mrs. Redburn's curiosity.

" What have you been doing with that, Katy? " she asked. " Ah, I fear I was right. We have no money! Our business is gone! Alas, we have nothing to hope for! "

" Oh, no, mother, it is not half so bad as that! "

exclaimed Katy.   " I went up to Mrs. Gordon for the purpose of borrowing twenty dollars of her; I didn't want it to look like charity, so I was going to ask her to keep the watch till it was paid.   That's all, mother."

" And she refused? "

" No; she was not at home."

" But your money is not all gone? "

Katy wanted to say it was not, but her conscience would not let her practice deception.   She had the three dollars which she had just borrowed of Michael, and that was not all gone.   But this was not the question her mother asked, and it would be a lie to say the money was not all gone, when she fully understood the meaning of the question.   Perhaps it was for her mother's good to deceive her; but she had been taught to feel that she had no right to do evil that good might follow.

" It was all gone, but I borrowed three dollars," she replied, after a little hesitation.

" Of whom? "

" Of Michael."

" Who is he? "

" Mrs. Gordon's man."

" Oh, Katy! How could you do so? " sighed Mrs. Redburn.

" I couldn't help it, mother. He would make me take it;" and she gave all the particulars of her interview with Michael, and reviewed the considerations which had induced her to accept the loan.

" Perhaps you are right, Katy. My pride would not have let me borrow of a servant; but it is wicked for me to cherish such a pride. I try very hard to banish it."

" Don't talk any more now, mother. We are too poor to be too proud to accept a favor of one who is in a humble station," replied Katy.

" I don't know what will become of us," said Mrs. Redburn, as she turned her head away to hide the tears that flooded her eyes.

Katy took up the Bible that lay by the bed side, and turning to the twenty-third psalm, she read,

" The Lord is my Shepherd; I shall not want.   He maketh me to lie down in green pastures; he leadeth me beside the still waters."

" Go on, Katy; those words are real comfort," said Mrs. Redburn, drying her tears.   " I know it is wicked for me to repine."

Katy read the whole psalm, and followed it with others, which produced a healing influence upon her mother's mind, and she seemed to forget that the purse was empty, and that they had placed themselves under obligations to a servant.

The sufferer rested much better than usual that night, and Katy was permitted to sleep the greater part of the time—a boon which her exhausted frame very much needed.   About ten o'clock in the forenoon Michael paid her a visit, to inform her that Mrs. Gordon had just arrived, and that, when he mentioned her case, she had sent him down to request her immediate attendance; and that his mistress would have come herself, only she was so much fatigued by her journey.

Katy could not leave then, for she had no one to stay with her mother; but Mrs. Sneed could come in an hour. Michael hastened home with the intelligence that Mrs. Redburn was better, and Katy soon followed him.

CHAPTER XX.

MRS. GORDON FEELS FAINT, AND KATY ENTERS A NEW SPHERE.

On her arrival at Temple Street Katy was promptly admitted by Michael, and shown in the sitting room, where Mrs. Gordon and Grace were waiting for her.

"I was very sorry to hear that your mother is sick, Katy," said the former; "and I should have paid you a visit, instead of sending for you, if I had not been so much exhausted by my journey from Baltimore."

"You are very kind, ma'am."

"Did Dr. Flynch call upon you at the first of the month?"

"Yes, ma'am; and we paid the rent as usual," replied Katy.

"I am sorry you did so, Katy; you should have told him that you were not in a condition to pay the rent."

"I couldn't tell him so, he is so cold and cruel."

"I think you misjudge him, for he has a really kind heart, and would not have distressed you for all the world.   Besides, I told him he need not collect your rent any time when you did not feel ready. to pay it.   I hope he gave you no trouble?"

"No, ma'am; I didn't give him a chance, for I paid him as soon as he demanded it; though it took nearly all the money we had.   I hope you will excuse me, ma'am, but I haven't liked him since the trouble we had a year ago, when he accused my dear mother of telling a lie."

"Perhaps he was hasty."

"I forgive him, ma'am; but I can't help thinking he is a very wicked man," answered Katy, with considerable emphasis.

"I hope not so bad as that; for I am sure, if you had told him it was not convenient for you to pay

the rent, he would not have insisted. But you
want some assitance, Katy?"

"Yes, ma'am; that is, I want to borrow some
money," replied Katy, blushing deeply.

"That's just like you," interposed Grace, laughing. "I suppose you will want to give your note
this time."

"I don't care about giving a note, but I mean to
pay the money back again, every cent of it."

"And the interest too, I suppose."

"Yes," said Katy, though she had not a very
clear idea of the value of money as an article of
merchandise.

"Don't distress her, Grace; you forget that her
mother is very sick, and she cannot feel like listening to your pleasantries," said Mrs. Gordon.

"Forgive me, Katy," replied Grace tenderly.

Katy burst into tears, though she could not
exactly tell why. She was overcome with emotion
as the beautiful young lady took her hand and
looked so sorrowfully in her face. She was **not**

used to so much kindness, so much sympathy, so much love, for it seemed as though both Grace and her mother loved her—that their hearts beat with hers.

"Don't cry, Katy; I am sorry I said a word," pleaded Grace. "I would not have hurt your feelings for all the world."

"You did not hurt my feelings; you are so kind to me that I could not help crying. I suppose I am very silly."

"No, you are not, Katy; now dry up your tears, and tell us all about it," added Mrs. Gordon, in soothing tones. "How long has your mother been sick?"

"Almost two weeks."

"What ails her?"

"She has got a fever; but she is much better to-day. The doctor says she hasn't got it very bad; but she has been very sick, I think."

"Who takes care of her?"

"I do, ma'am."

"You! She must need a great deal of attention. But who takes care of her at night?"

"I do, ma'am. I have been up a great deal every night."

"Poor child! It is enough to wear you out."

"I wouldn't mind it at all, if I had nothing else to trouble me."

"What other troubles have you?"

"I can't make any candy now, and haven't made any for nearly a fortnight; so that we have no money coming in. We spent nearly all we had in buying our winter clothing and fuel. It worries me very much, for we had plenty of money before mother was taken sick."

"I hope you haven't wanted for anything."

"No, ma'am; for when my purse was empty I came up here, only yesterday, to borrow some of you, if you would please to lend it to me."

"Certainly I will, my child. I am very glad you came."

"Michael would make me tell what I wanted,

and then he let me have three dollars, and offered to let me have as much as I wanted.   I didn't know as you would like it if I borrowed money of your servant."

" You did just right; and I am glad that Michael has a kind heart.   Now, how much money do you want? "

" I thought I would ask you to lend me twenty dollars; and just as soon, after mother gets well, as I can gather the money together, I will pay you— and the interest," she added, glancing at Grace.

" Now, Katy, that is too bad! " exclaimed Grace, catching her by the hand, while a tear started from her eye.   " You know I didn't mean that."

" I know you didn't; but I don't know much about such things, and thought likely it was right for us to pay interest if we borrowed money."

" I should be very glad to give you twenty dollars, Katy, if you would only let me; for I am rich, as well as mother; and I certainly should not think of taking interest."

"We will say no more about that," interrupted Mrs. Gordon. "I will let you have the money with the greatest pleasure, for I know you will make good use of it."

"I will, indeed."

"And you must promise me that you will not distress yourself to pay it again," continued the kind lady, as she took out her purse.

"I will not distress myself, but I will pay it as soon as I can."

"You must not be too proud."

"No, ma'am; but just proud enough."

"Yes, that's it," replied Mrs. Gordon, smiling. "Pride is a very good thing in its place. It keeps people from being mean and wicked sometimes."

"That's true pride," added Katy.

"Yes; for there is a false pride, which makes people very silly and vain; which keeps them from doing their duty very often. You have none of this kind of pride."

"I hope not."

" Your friend Simon Sneed, whom the mayor spoke to me about, affords us a very good example of the folly of cherishing false pride. Where is Simon now? "

" He keeps in a store in Washington Street; he is a salesman now, and I don't think he is so foolish as he was."

" Perhaps the lesson he learned did him good. But I am keeping you away from your mother, Katy. Who stays at home with her while you are away? "

" Mrs. Sneed—Simon's mother."

" Then she is a good woman."

" And Simon is very kind; he has done a great many things for me, and I hope I shall be able to do something for him one of these days."

" That's right, Katy. Think well of your friends, though others speak ill of them," said Grace. " Ah, there comes the carriage. I am going home with you, Katy, to see your mother."

" You are very kind, Miss Grace."

" Here is the money," added Mrs. Gordon, handing her a little roll of bills.

"Thank you, ma'am," replied Katy, as she placed the money in her portemonnaie.   " But——"

Here she came to a full stop, and her face was as crimson as a blush rose; but she took out the silver watch, and approached Mrs. Gordon.

" What were you going to say, Katy?"

" I brought this watch up," stammered she.

" What for?"

" You know I am a poor girl; my mother is a poor woman, and we didn't want you to think you were giving us the money, for we are very proud; that is, my mother is very proud, and so am I; and——"

Here Katy drew a long breath, and came to a full stop again, unable to say what she wanted to say.

" If you want anything else, Katy, don't hesitate to mention it; for I will not do anything to mortify your pride, even if it is unreasonable," said Mrs.

Gordon. " I understand you perfectly; the twenty dollars is not a gift, but a loan."

" Yes, ma'am; but if we should never be able to pay it, then it would be a gift."

" No, it wouldn't."

" I think so; and so I brought this watch, which you will please to take as security for the payment of the loan," said Katy, much confused, as she offered the watch to Mrs. Gordon.

"My dear child, I do not want any security. Your word is just as good as your bond."

" But I would rather you would take it. My mother is prouder than I am, for she wasn't always as poor as she is now."

Katy suddenly clapped her hand over her mouth, when she recollected that this was a forbidden topic.

" Some time you may tell me all about your mother; and I will call and see her to-morrow, and help you take care of her."

" Please to take the watch, ma'am."

"If you very much desire it, I shall do so, though I cannot take it as a security. Is this the watch you carried to the pawnbroker?" said Mrs. Gordon as she took the treasure.

"Yes, ma'am. It belonged to my father."

Mrs. Gordon turned over the watch, and looked at it with considerable interest, as she thought of it as a memento of the dead, and how highly it must be prized by the poor woman.

"Mercy! what's this!" exclaimed she, starting back, and staggering toward her chair.

"What is the matter, mother?" cried Grace, running to her side. "Are you ill?"

"No, Grace; that inscription!" replied Mrs. Gordon faintly, for she seemed very deeply moved, and on the point of swooning. "Bring me a glass of water."

There was no water in the room, but Michael was in the entry, and was dispatched to procure it. He returned in a moment, and when Mrs. Gordon had in some measure recovered from the sudden shock, she pointed to the inscription on the back of the watch:

" M. G.
to
J. R.
All for the Best."

" What does it mean, mother?   I do not see **any** thing very strange about that."

" I have seen this watch before," she replied, stopping to think.   " Where did your mother get this watch, Katy?" she asked, as it occurred to her that she might be arriving at a conclusion too suddenly.

" It was my father's."

" Where did your father get it?   Did you ever hear your mother say?"

" Yes, ma'am; her father, who was a rich Liverpool merchant, gave it to her husband, my father," replied Katy, who felt justified in revealing what her mother had told her to keep secret.

" Mercy!" gasped Mrs. Gordon, almost overcome by her emotions.

"What is the matter, mother? What has **all** this to do with you?" asked Grace anxiously.

"Come here, Katy, my child," continued **Mrs.** Gordon, as she drew the little candy merchant to her side, and warmly embraced her. "Your mother, Katy, is my sister, I have scarcely a doubt."

"Why, mother! Is it possible?" exclaimed Grace.

"It is even so. Mrs. Redburn, whose name we have often heard mentioned without thinking it might be the wife of John Redburn, my father's clerk, is my sister. I had given her up, and have regarded her as dead for more than ten years. But, Grace, get my things, and I will go to her at once."

"Is that your portrait, ma'am?" asked Katy, wistfully, pointing to the picture of the mischievous lady.

"No, child; that is your mother's portrait."

"I almost knew it."

"It was taken when **she was** only sixteen years

old.   She was a gay, wild girl then.   I suppose she is sadly changed now."

The thought completely overcame Mrs. Gordon, and throwing herself upon a sofa, she wept like a child.   She thought of her sister suffering from poverty and want, while she had been rolling in opulence and plenty.   Grace tried to comfort her, but it was some time before she was in a condition to enter the carriage which was waiting at the door.

"What an adventure, mother!" exclaimed Grace, as she seated herself by the side of Katy; and it was evident she had a vein of the romantic in her composition.

"Do not talk to me, Grace.   My heart is too full for words."

"But I may talk to Katy—may I not?"

"Yes."

"Well, cousin Katy," laughed Grace; "I shall call you cousin, though you are not really my cousin."

"Not your cousin?" said Katy, a shade of disappointment crossing her animated features.

"No; for Mrs. Gordon is not really my mother; only my stepmother; but she is just as good as a real mother, for I never knew any other. Dear me! how strange all this is! And you will go up and live with us in Temple Street, and——"

"I can't leave my mother," interrupted Katy.

"Your mother shall go too."

"She is too sick now."

Grace continued to talk as fast as she could, laying out ever so many plans for the future, till the carriage reached Colvin Court. I will not follow them into the chamber of the sick woman, where Mrs. Gordon, by a slow process that did not agitate the invalid too violently, revealed herself to her sister. The fine lady of Temple Street had a heart, a warm and true heart, and not that day, nor that night, nor for a week, did she leave the sick bed of the sufferer. There, in the midst of her sister's poverty, she did a sister's offices.

It was three weeks before Mrs. Redburn was in a condition to be moved to her sister's house; and then she was once more in the midst of the luxury and splendor of her early life. One day, when she had improved so much as to be able to bear the fatigue of a long conversation, Mrs. Gordon, who had thus far declined to discuss any exciting topics with the invalid, proposed to have everything explained. Each had a very long story to tell; but as the reader already knows Mrs. Redburn's history, I shall only briefly narrate that of Mrs. Gordon and the Guthrie family, after the departure of the former.

Mr. Guthrie, the father of both, died two years after the flight of Margaret,—Mrs. Redburn,—when of course there was a large property to be divided. Diligent search was made for Margaret in America, but her husband had declared to some person in Liverpool that he had an engagement in Montreal. This place was thoroughly canvassed, but without success. No trace of the runaways could be discovered. Agents were sent to various parts of America, and no tidings of Margaret had ever reached them.

About two years after her father's death, Jane—Mrs. Gordon—had married a very wealthy gentleman from Baltimore. He was then a widower with one child—Grace Gordon. She had come to America with him, and resided in Baltimore till his death, a period of only two years. Then, having never liked to live in that city, she had removed to Boston, where she had a few friends. She had invested her money and resided there, very happily situated, and with no desire to return to her native land.

Her father's estate had been divided, and the portion which belonged to Margaret was held in trust for seven years,—when the law presumed she was dead,—and it was then delivered to her sister, who was the only living heir. Now that the younger sister had appeared, it was promptly paid over to her, and Mrs. Redburn, before poor and proud, was now rich, and humility never sat more gracefully on the brow of woman than on hers.

Katy and her mother had entered upon a new life, and in the midst of luxury and splendors they could not forget the past, nor cease to thank God for his past and present mercies. Mrs. Gordon used to declare it was strange she had never thought that Mrs. Redburn might be her sister, but it was declared that stranger things than that had happened.

Katy continued to go to school with great regularity, and became an excellent scholar. She was beloved by all her companions, and Grace, who was married shortly after Katy entered the family, always regarded her with the affection of a sister, insisting that she should spend half the time at her house. Mrs. Redburn was soon completely restored to health. She had a fortune to manage now, and when Dr. Flynch proposed to her to collect her rents and take charge of her affairs, she respectfully declined the offer. Mrs. Gordon did not like him as well as formerly, for her sister had opened her eyes in regard to his true character, and she soon found an opportunity to discharge him.

Having carried Katy through her principal troubles, and chronicled the rise and fall of the candy trade, we shall step forward ten years to take a final look at her and her friends, and then bid them farewell.

CHAPTER XXI.

KATY GOES TO CHURCH, AND HAS A BIRTHDAY PARTY.

TEN years is a long time—long enough to change the child into a woman, the little candy merchant into a fine lady. I suppose, therefore, that my young friends will need to be introduced to Miss Redburn. There she sits in the pleasant apartment in Temple Street, where the picture of the mischievous girl still hangs, though it looks very little like the matron at her side, for whom it was taken. She is not beautiful enough to be the heroine of a romance, neither has she done any absurd thing; she has only supported her mother when she had no one else to care for her. But Katy is irresistible if she is not pretty. She still looks as pleasant as a morning in June, and smiles sweetly when anyone speaks to her and when she speaks to anyone.

I am sorry I cannot inform my young lady friends how Miss Redburn was dressed, or how she proposed to dress, at her birthday party, which was to come off the following week—what silks, what laces, what muslins, and what jewels she was to wear. I can only say that she was dressed very plainly, and that her garments were exceedingly becoming; and that she had steadily resisted the solicitations of sundry French milliners and dress-makers to exceed her usual simplicity at the party, and I cordially commend her example to all young ladies.

While Miss Redburn sat at the window, the door bell rang with great violence, and Michael—yes, Michael—he is still there, a veteran in the service of Mrs. Gordon, and fully believing that Katy is an angel—Michael hastened to admit Grace. She is a little older than when we saw her last, but she is the same Grace. She enters the room, kisses Katy with as much zeal as though she had not seen her for a month, though they had met the day before. She had scarcely saluted her cousin before a little fat man of six came tumbling into the room, for he had not been able to keep up with his mother.

"Come, aunty," said little Tommy, who persisted in calling her by this title, as he rolled up to Miss Redburn, who gave him a hearty kiss—"come, aunty, I want you to come right down into the kitchen, and make me a lot of molatheth candy."

"Not now, Tommy"—would you believe it, reader? that little boy's name is Thomas Howard Parker—"not now, Tommy. I came to tell you, Katy, that the King of the Billows has been telegraphed."

"Has she?" exclaimed Katy, a deep blush suffusing her cheek.

"Yes; and you must go right down to the wharf, or we shall not be in season to see Captain Howard, who is coming up in a pilot boat."

Miss Redburn hastened to put on her things, and she and Mrs. Parker seated themselves in the carriage that waited them.

Of course you know Captain Howard, reader? He has followed the seas only eleven years; and though but twenty-five years old, he is the commander of a fine clipper, and sails in the Liverpool line. He is frequently quoted as an example of what patient perseverance will accomplish; for, with very little aid from friends, he has worked his way from the forecastle into the cabin. He is a self-educated man, and has won for himself the reputation of being a thorough sailor and a perfect gentleman.

Pursuant to a little arrangement made between Captain Howard and Miss Redburn, just as he departed on his voyage, they were both seen in church on the following Thursday afternoon; and when they came out people addressed Katy as Mrs. Howard. But to pass on to the occasion which she had chosen to call a birthday party, though it was not exactly that; and as it came immediately after the church service, some called it a levee.

There are a great many persons in the Gordon mansion, as many as two hundred, I should think. Of course I cannot stop to introduce all of them, but there are a few who deserve this favor.

"Mr. Sneed, I am delighted to see you," said Mrs. Howard, as a very tall and very slim gentleman, elegantly dressed, approached.

"You do me honor, madam. It is the superlative felicity of my sublunary existence to congratulate you on this auspicious occasion," replied Mr. Sneed, as he gently pressed the gloved hand of the lady.

That sounds just like Master Simon Sneed, only very much intensified. Simon is a salesman still, in a large establishment—has never risen above that position, and probably never will; for, born to be a gentleman, he feels as much above his business as his business really is above him.

Simon's father and mother say a pleasant word

to the bride, and pass on.   And here comes a great fat woman, whose tongue flies like the shuttle in a loom.   Well, it is the captain's mother.   Since her son has been prosperous she has had an easy time of it, and has grown very corpulent.

"Who do you think has come, Katy?" puffed Mrs. Howard.

"I don't know.   Who?"

"Mrs. Colvin, that was! Mrs. McCarty, that is."

Some of the very good-natured people laughed, and some of the very fastidious ones turned up their noses when they saw Mrs. McCarty so warmly received by the bride; but she did not care who laughed or who sneered, she was not too proud to welcome, in the hour of prosperity and happiness, those who had been her friends in adversity.

"Mrs. Howard, I congratulate you," said a fat man, who was puffing and blowing at the heat of the room.

It was an ex-mayor; and after he had said a few pleasant words he passed on to make room for a hundred more who were waiting to speak to the bride.

That was a very pleasant party, but as we are opposed to crowded rooms and late hours, we may as well retire.

The next day the happy couple started upon a bridal tour, and on their return Captain Howard sailed for Liverpool, in his fine ship, with Mrs. Howard as a passenger.

And now, my young friends, adieu. If you are poor, don't be too proud to work at any honest occupation; but be too proud to do wrong—too proud to degrade yourself in your own eyes, by doing a mean act, and in this sense you may truly be " Poor and Proud."

THE END.

THE FAMOUS
HENTY BOOKS
The Boys' Own Library
12mo, Cloth

G. A. Henty has long held the field as the most popular boys' author. Age after age of heroic deeds has been the subject of his pen, and the knights of old seem very real in his pages. Always wholesome and manly, always heroic and of high ideals, his books are more than popular wherever the English language is spoken.

Each volume is printed on excellent paper from new large-type plates, bound in cloth, assorted colors, with an attractive ink and gold stamp. **Price 30 Cents.**

A Final Reckoning
    A Tale of Bush Life in Australia
Among the Malay Pirates
By England's Aid
    The Freeing of the Netherlands
By Right of Conquest
    A Tale of Cortez in Mexico
Bravest of the Brave
    A Tale of Peterborough in Spain
By Pike and Dyke
    The Rise of the Dutch Republic
By Sheer Pluck
    A Tale of the Ashantee War
Bonnie Prince Charlie
    A Tale of Fontenoy and Culloden
Captain Bayley's Heir
    A Tale of the Gold Fields of California
Cat of Bubastes
    A Story of Ancient Egypt
Colonel Thorndyke's Secret
Cornet of Horse
    A Tale of Marlborough's Wars
Facing Death
    A Tale of the Coal Mines
Friends, though Divided
    A Tale of the Civil War in England
For Name and Fame
    A Tale of Afghan Warfare
For the Temple
    A Tale of the Fall of Jerusalem
In Freedom's Cause
    A Story of Wallace and Bruce
In the Reign of Terror
    The Adventures of a Westminster Boy
In Times of Peril   A Tale of India
Jack Archer   A Tale of the Crimea
Lion of St. Mark
    A Tale of Venice in the XIV. Century
Lion of the North
    A Tale of Gustavus Adolphus

Maori and Settler
    A Tale of the New Zealand War
Orange and Green
    A Tale of the Boyne and Limerick
One of the 28th   A Tale of Waterloo
Out on the Pampas
    A Tale of South America
Rujub the Juggler
St. George for England
    A Tale of Crécy and Poictiers
Sturdy and Strong
True to the Old Flag
    A Tale of the Revolution
The Golden Cañon
The Lost Heir
The Young Colonists
    A Tale of the Zulu and Boer War
The Young Midshipman
The Dragon and the Raven
    A Tale of King Alfred
The Boy Knight
    A Tale of the Crusades
Through the Fray
    A Story of the Luddite Riots
Under Drake's Flag
    A Tale of the Spanish Main
With Wolfe in Canada
    The Tale of Winning a Continent
With Clive in India
    The Beginning of an Empire
With Lee in Virginia
    A Story of the American Civil War
Young Carthaginian
    A Story of the Times of Hannibal
Young Buglers
    A Tale of the Peninsular War
Young Franc-Tireurs
    A Tale of the Franco-Prussian War

THE MERSHON COMPANY

298 Fifth Ave., New York   Rahway, N. J.

FLAG OF FREEDOM SERIES

By CAPTAIN RALPH BONEHILL

**Volumes Illustrated, Bound in Cloth, with a very Attractive Cover,
Price 60 Cents per Volume**

WITH CUSTER IN THE BLACK HILLS; or, A Young Scout among the Indians

This is a complete story in itself, but forms the sixth and last volume of Captain Bonehill's popular "Flag of Freedom" Series. It tells of the remarkable experiences of a youth who, with his parent, goes to the Black Hills in search of gold. Custer's last battle is well described. A volume every lad fond of Indian stories should possess.

BOYS OF THE FORT; or, A Young Captain's Pluck

Captain Bonehill is at his best when relating a tale of military adventure, and this story of stirring doings at one of our well-known forts in the Wild West is of more than ordinary interest. The young captain had a difficult task to accomplish, but he had been drilled to do his duty, and he did it thoroughly. Gives a good insight into army life of to-day.

THE YOUNG BANDMASTER; or, Concert Stage and Battlefield

In this tale Captain Bonehill touches upon a new field. The hero is a youth with a passion for music, who, compelled to make his own way in the world, becomes a cornetist in an orchestra, and works his way up, first, to the position of a soloist, and then to that of leader of a brass band. He is carried off to sea and falls in with a secret-service cutter bound for Cuba, and while in that island joins a military band which accompanies our soldiers in the never-to-be-forgotten attack on Santiago. A mystery connected with the hero's inheritance adds to the interest of the tale.

OFF FOR HAWAII; or, The Mystery of a Great Volcano

Here we have fact and romance cleverly interwoven. Several boys start on a tour of the Hawaiian Islands. They have heard that there is a treasure located in the vicinity of Kilauea, the largest active volcano in the world, and go in search of it. Their numerous adventures will be followed with much interest.

A SAILOR BOY WITH DEWEY; or, Afloat in the Philippines

The story of Dewey's victory in Manila Bay will never grow old, but here we have it told in a new form—not as those in command witnessed the contest, but as it appeared to a real, live American youth who was in the navy at the time. Many adventures in Manila and in the interior follow, giving true-to-life scenes from this remote portion of the globe. A book that should be in every boy's library.

WHEN SANTIAGO FELL; or, The War Adventures of Two Chums

Captain Bonehill has never penned a better tale than this stirring story of adventures in Cuba. Two boys, an American and his Cuban chum, leave New York to join their parents in the interior of Cuba. The war between Spain and the Cubans is on, and the boys are detained at Santiago de Cuba, but escape by crossing the bay at night. Many adventures between the lines follow, and a good pen-picture of General Garcia is given. The American lad, with others, is captured and cast into a dungeon in Santiago; and then follows the never-to-be-forgotten campaign in Cuba under General Shafter. How the hero finally escapes makes reading no wide-awake boy will want to miss.

Press Opinions of Captain Bonehill's Books for Boys

"Captain Bonehill's stories will always be popular with our boys, for the reason that they are thoroughly up-to-date and true to life. As a writer of outdoor tales he has no rival."—*Bright Days.*

---

(2)   **THE MERSHON COMPANY**

156 Fifth Ave., New York   **Rahway, N. J.**

MRS. L. T. MEADE'S
FAMOUS BOOKS FOR GIRLS

12mo, Cloth • **Price 60 cents**

There are few more favorite authors with American girls than Mrs. L. T. MEADE, whose copyright works can only be had from us. Essentially a writer for the home, with the loftiest aims and purest sentiments, Mrs. Meade's books possess the merit of utility as well as the means of amusement. They are girls' books—written for girls, and fitted for every home.

Here will be found no maudlin nonsense as to the affections. There are no counts in disguise nor castles in Spain. It is pure and wholesome literature of a high order with a lofty ideal.

The volumes are all copyright, excellently printed with clear, open type, uniformly bound in best cloth, with ink and gold stamp.

THE FOLLOWING ARE THE TITLES

The Children of Wilton Chase	A World of Girls
Bashful Fifteen	Good Luck
Betty: A Schoolgirl	A Girl in Ten Thousand
Four on an Island	A Young Mutineer
Girls New and Old	Wild Kitty
Out of the Fashion	The Children's Pilgrimage
The Palace Beautiful	The Girls of St. Wode's
Polly, a New-Fashioned Girl	Light o' the Morning
Red Rose and Tiger Lily	Bad Little Hannah
Temptation of Olive Latimer	Rebellion of Lil Carrington
A Ring of Rubies	A Little Mother to the Others
A Sweet Girl Graduate	Merry Girls of England
Bunch of Cherries	Daddy's Girl

The Time of Roses

---

(3) **THE MERSHON COMPANY**

156 Fifth Ave., New York　　　　　　　　　**Rahway, N. J**

NEW JUVENILES

By Famous Authors

*Bound in Cloth; decorated cover designs; printed on extra book paper;
burnished colored edges; handsomely illustrated.*

THE MANOR SCHOOL. By Mrs. L. T. Meade. Ten Full-Page Illustrations.

A sweetly written and popular story of girl life. Full of fun and adventure. Told in a manner to interest and amuse young people of any age.
Very few authors have achieved a popularity equal to that of Mrs. Meade as a writer of stories for girls. Her characters are living beings of flesh and blood. Into the trials and crosses of these the reader enters at once with zest and hearty sympathy. Mrs. Meade always writes with a high moral purpose. Cloth. 12mo. Price, $1.25.

THE DEFENSE OF THE CASTLE. A Story for Boys and Girls. By Tudor Jenks, author of " Imaginotions," "World's Fair Book," "Boys' Book of Explorations," "Galopoff, the Talking Pony," "Gypsy, the Talking Dog," etc.

This is a good, lively, fighting story, but not bloodthirsty. It tells of a boy and girl who, during the absence of their father at the Crusades, with the help of an old soldier defended the castle from the attack of an armed force led by a treacherous relative. The time is about that of Ivanhoe. Cloth. 12mo. Price, $1.00.

WITH BOONE ON THE FRONTIER; or, The Pioneer Boys of Old Kentucky. By Captain Ralph Bonehill.

This tale is complete in itself, but forms Volume I of the " Frontier Series." It relates the true-to-life adventures of two boys who, in company with their folks, move westward with Daniel Boone. Contains many thrilling scenes among the Indians and encounters with wild animals. Written in Captain Bonehill's best style, and will most likely be the boys' book of the season. Cloth. 12mo. Price, $1.00.

UNDER THE STAR-SPANGLED BANNER. Story of a Boy's Adventures in the Spanish-American War. By Captain F. S. Brereton, author of " Dragon of Pekin," etc.

A vivid and accurate account of this memorable struggle. The hero leaves his home in search of work, finds it on a Cuban plantation, is denounced to the Spaniards as a spy, makes his escape to the American fleet, and afterwards joins the Rough Riders and participates in the battles around Santiago. Cloth. 12mo. Price, $1.00.

THE MERSHON COMPANY, RAHWAY, N. J.

The Famous Andrew Lang Fairy Books

✤ ✤ ✤

The Blue, Red, Green, and Yellow Fairy Books

12mo.   Price 60 cents per volume, postpaid

Never were there more popular books of Fairy Tales than these famous collections made by Andrew Lang. At his able hands the romantic literature of the world has been laid under contribution. The folk-lore of Ireland, the romance of the Rhine, and the wild legends of the west coast of Scotland, with all the glamour and mystery of the Scottish border, have contributed to this famous series of fairy tales.

Here are the tales that have delighted generations of children, some culled from old English versions of the eighteenth century, some modernized from quaint chap-books, and all handsomely and modernly illustrated. With the aid of a scholar such as Mr. Lang, the entire world has contributed to this famous series. There is material here for years of delight for children.

Each volume is profusely illustrated, printed on velvet-finished paper, bound in cloth, with a very attractive stamp in ink and gold.

These books should be read in the following order : 1, The Blue Fairy Book ; 2, The Red Fairy Book ; 3, The Green Fairy Book; 4, The Yellow Fairy Book.

| The Blue Fairy Book | The Green Fairy Book |
| The Red Fairy Book | The Yellow Fairy Book |

www.ingramcontent.com/pod-product-compliance
Lightning Source LLC
Chambersburg PA
CBHW031036120726
47905CB00007B/2212